SMOKE & MIRRORS

THE HUNTERS - BOOK 2

RORI BLEU

ROSIE CHAPEL

Smoke & Mirrors

The Hunters - Book 2
A Dystopian Yarn

by

Rori Bleu & Rosie Chapel

First printing: 2024
ISBN: 978-1-7635407-9-8 (ebook)
ISBN: 978-1-7637753-0-5 (paperback)

Ulfire Pty. Ltd.
P.O. Box 1481
South Perth
WA 6951
Australia

Cover Design: Rebecca Norman
Images Courtesy: Canva.
Designed in Canva using appropriate licences.

Created with Vellum

1

Sophia muttered balefully as she wove her way through the increasingly cramped confines of the caravan. What had always seemed a spacious abode, had taken on the dimensions of a bird's nest the closer she came to term.

Spying the anatomy volume she sought, perched precariously on the shelf at the opposite end of the caravan where her mother's medical tomes were stored, Sophia squeezed between the table and the counter.

"Gods," she swore loudly as her swollen belly struck the edge of the table.

In response, the baby curled inside Sophia demonstrated his… or her… displeasure with an emphatic foot.

She rubbed her stomach, placating, "I'm sorry I woke you. Mind, it's only fair given you take great delight in keeping me up all night."

"Is that any way to speak to an unborn?" Nicoletta chuckled, entering Sophia's caravan unannounced and uninvited.

Sophia glowered at her head of personal security, which

became a black scowl when the woman helped herself to Sophia's cup of tea and breakfast.

Preparing to deliver a thorough tongue-lashing for sheer impudence, Sophia spied Nicoletta's three-year-old twins tagging along behind her.

The sight prompted Sophia to soften her mood... marginally.

"Please, help yourself. I think there might be some weapons you can filch, as well."

Nicoletta smiled and shook her head, "Nah, I've already checked. Those pieces of scrap metal you called daggers—"

"*Called*?" Sophia interjected silkily.

Nicoletta ignored the question, "I sent to the smithy to be melted down into screws."

"How kind of you," Sophia huffed. "So, pray tell, to what do I owe the privilege of your company this morning? Perhaps you wish to scrap my caravan as well?"

Putting up a hand to freeze her friend's questions in front of little ears with large mouths, Nicoletta gave her children a muffin each. "Alright you two, go find your father. It's his turn to entertain you, and if he says he's too busy, tell him Mama will set the evil padrona on him."

Devouring their treat, the pair giggled and waved to the leader of their camp, bidding her, "Bye, bye, Auntie Softy."

Zara and Rocco had bestowed this nickname on Sophia almost as soon as they could talk, although Sophia reckoned it was a moniker picked up from their mother who rarely missed an opportunity to tease her boss about losing her edge.

Nevertheless, Sophia played along, growling playfully like a bear, swiping a paw at the two.

That sent them tumbling out of the door, squealing with laughter, and racing to the protection of their father and their caravan.

Wincing at the slam of the screen door, certain they would knock the dilapidated thing off its hinges one day, Sophia asked her trusted guard casually, "How did you survive having two of those creatures inside you?"

"And in a smaller caravan no less," Nicoletta sallied, draining the remnants of the tea.

"Do not complain to me about the size of your place. In case you have forgotten, I was the one who suggested you and Dante find a new one."

"Easier said than done, my dearest Padrona," Nicoletta scoffed. "I cannot recall the last traveling caravan salesman who happened through our camp. Oh wait… there he is on your wall."

"Well, I did not like the range of caravans he offered, or his pricing, and why are you still banging on about it? That was three years ago. You've had plenty of time to drag Dante out to look for a new one?"

"Do not get me started on my man right now and the things he should be doing." A flicker of irritation soured Nicoletta's normally sunny demeanour.

Discretion being the better part of valour, Sophia chose not to intervene, aware of the depth of affection the pair shared and that each would face death to protect the other.

Unexpectedly, scenes from the raid on Rome flashed through Sophia's mind, an unwelcome reminder. The camp had lost too many of their numbers that night.

Sophia also realised the peace hammered out between herself and the Roman chancellor, Callixtus, may have instigated the current apathy exhibited by her warriors. On top of that, lack of conflict with their city dwelling neighbours had, no doubt, contributed to the increase of Bacchanalian frivolity.

Too much wine, not enough work! Her mother, Noemi, the

late padrona of the camp, whispered disdainfully in Sophia's ear.

Ghosts were one thing, a chastising revenant only Sophia could see was something else. Her mother meant well, but she always picked the worst times to be annoying.

"Shush," Sophia grouched.

"Excuse me?" Nicoletta shot back, startled.

"Huh?" Sophia countered, her expression one of confusion.

"Why did you just shush me? I didn't say anything."

"No… not you," Sophia tried to explain, to see her mother shaking her head smugly.

Exasperated at the three-way conversation, despite one being spectral, Sophia deflected with a question of her own, "Why are you here again?"

Eyeing her friend and leader warily, Nicoletta attributed Sophia's odd behaviour to her pregnancy. Ignoring it, she replied, "I thought you might be interested to know our advanced scouts in the north are not back yet."

"How long have they been absent?"

"They should have returned before dusk last night."

Snatching the last of her breakfast from the head of her security's reach, Sophia popped it in her mouth, mumbling around the morsel, "Do you think it necessary to be alarmed? They are only half a day late. Besides, if I know Isabel and Enzo, they are probably in some hayloft—"

"Padrona," a title by which Nicoletta addressed Sophia when she planned to admonish her, "do you take your duties so lightly? What would your mother… rest her soul… say if she saw you right now?"

Sophia did not need to guess. She saw Noemi curl her translucent fists and plant them angrily on her hips, umbrage clear on her face.

Sophia sighed. "My apologies, Nic. I spoke in haste. What

do you suggest?" The tension between the two eased at Sophia's use of the diminutive.

"I would like to take Dante and search for them."

"Normally, I would agree without hesitation, but what about your kids? You cannot think it's sensible to take them with you."

"Give me some credit," Nicoletta said with an evil grin, knowing Sophia had just stepped into her trap. "I assumed their auntie would volunteer to watch them. They *are* little angels after all."

"Angels, riiiiiight," Sophia drawled wryly then raised her palm. "And don't look at me. I can barely waddle, never mind chase down your boisterous pair."

"Isn't Bianca coming today?" Nicoletta was the picture of innocence.

Amused at her friend's audacity, Sophia smirked. "Ha, you are braver than I, but have at it. Mind, she'll be busy teaching the midwives, hands-on experience with your little monsters might prove beneficial."

She sobered and canted her head at Nicoletta. "When do you want to set out?"

"As soon as possible." Nicoletta experienced a twinge of guilt for springing her plan on Sophia.

"Why does that not surprise me?" Sophia rolled her eyes and was about to add something when her shrewd brain went into overdrive.

Suppressing an almost irresistible urge to slap the unrepentant smile off her chief of security's face, Sophia wagged a finger. "Now, just hang on a cotton-pickin' minute, Bianca isn't due until late afternoon. You expect *me* to ask her?"

"Come, on, just a small favour…" Nicoletta wheedled.

"*Small favour*?" Sophia's tone went up an octave, making Nicoletta wince. "Bianca has no chance of saying no. That's pretty sneaky if you ask me. How am I supposed to entertain Zara and Rocco for a whole day?"

"We…ll," Nicoletta drew out the word, as two deep creases puckered Sophia's brow. "You could think of it as practice."

That was when Sophia gave Nicoletta's left cheek a solid wack… just because her friend deserved it.

Rubbing her jaw, Nicoletta chuckled, "Is that a yes then?"

"As long as those two know I will feed them to the wolves if they misbehave."

Once she had received the padrona's… grudging… blessing to dump her little darlings on Bianca, Nicoletta beat a hasty retreat to her caravan, to collect her mate before Sophia had the chance to reconsider or take a second swing.

Rounding the corner of their home, Nicoletta came to a flabbergasted halt at the sight of Dante stretched out on a hammock; their two children tethered to trees far enough apart to keep them out of his, and each other's, reach.

Hearing the crunch of boots on gravel, the twins turned. Imminent squeals of delight at the arrival of their mother, arrested by Nicoletta's quick finger to her lips.

Drawing her blade from its sheath, Nicoletta crept to her husband, cutting the children loose as she approached.

Freed, the twins resumed their brawl under the watchful eye of their mother, which ended up on top of their father, overturning the hammock.

"Dammit, you two," Dante growled at them, "How in the hell did you free yourselves?"

The response — riotous laughter.

Clearing her throat to get her loving mate's attention, Nicoletta grouched, "Get your lazy keister up."

"Keister?" The twins danced around, singing, "Keister. Keister. Papa has a keister."

Shaking his head at his offspring, Dante asked his wife, "To what do I owe this rude awakening?"

Nicoletta sighed. "If harnessing your children like two wild forest creatures—"

"If the cap fits," Dante interrupted slyly.

"Do not even go there. As I was saying, if tying our kids to trees was not reason enough, I have urgent need of your help. Please take these two to Sophia's caravan, then get your ass back here so we can head north. I've volunteered you and I to be a search party, and do not start complaining."

"Would not think of it, my love." Dante brushed a kiss to her bruised cheek. "I'm not one to look a gift horse in the mouth. Mind," he waggled his brows comically, "I do feel a smidge of pity for our dearest padrona who, I'll wager, will never agree to babysitting our little poppets again."

That earned him a non-lethal slash from Nicoletta's blade as she chased him away.

2

"I still say you are being overly cautious, mí amor," Dante griped for the umpteenth time as the couple relied on the grey gloom of the pending nightfall for cover.

After following the Via Braccianese Claudia — once an ancient route connecting Rome to the lakes of Bracciano and Martignano, now a motorway empty of traffic — on foot for two long days they had come upon the ruined village of Farniole, an outpost on the border of Hunters' lands.

The ghostly enclave was dotted with decaying husks of hotels and villas which once had welcomed tourists.

Without acknowledging Dante's grating reprise of an opinion, repeated since they left the camp, Nicoletta decided to call it a night and shelter in the first vaguely habitable, if brooding, inn they came across.

Anything was better than listening to his continual whinging, she thought, rubbing her throbbing temples.

Sliding down the embankment next to the nearest building, Nicoletta headed inside without waiting for Dante.

Making her way through the cobweb strewn lobby, she climbed the rickety staircase to the first floor. She heard Dante behind her but ignored him, her focus on finding a room which still sported windowpanes.

By the time Nicoletta shoved her way through the fifth door, Dante had caught up.

Traipsing over the threshold, she tossed her pack on the bed. The room reeked of mould and mildew, but she was too exhausted from the search, and her husband, to look for a less unpalatable refuge.

Sitting on the edge of the bed, Nicoletta studied Dante who had his back to her as he unpacked the necessary supplies for the night from his rucksack.

She knew every inch of his chiselled body, and the scarcely discernible hunch of his usually straight shoulders, spoke volumes. It was as though his reason to live had deserted him.

Wearily, she muttered with a frown, "What happened to my headstrong mate, the one who charged defiantly into the fray against the Romans? Since the twins' birth, all you have done is lounge about. I cannot coerce you into battle like we used to. Even now, you have done nothing but whine like a child since we left the encampment."

Dante froze at her accusation.

He sank against the worn bureau and stretched out to grab a neatly wrapped sandwich, tossing it to Nicoletta, while he contemplated a suitable answer.

Snagging a bottle of water, the source of his apathy struck him square between the eyes, and he almost smacked his forehead, stunned it had taken him so long to realise.

He did not like admitting fault, but knew, in this, he had no choice. Nicoletta was too important to him. He began diffidently, "*Mí amor,* since the truce, I have struggled to adapt, you know that. It's like the rug has been pulled out from under me and I'm floundering to find my feet again," he paused and a faint flush crept up his cheeks as he, circuitously, came to the crux of the matter. "What use am I to you?"

Nicoletta's jaw nearly hit the floor at this confession. "What on Earth do you mean? Where did that rubbish come from? How could you possibly believe such a thing?" Her tone incredulous.

"You have a purpose, Nic. Not only are you the mother of our children, but you're also the padrona's chief of security."

Taking a deep breath, Dante tried to explain, "You are Sophia's right-hand. She relies on you. You have an important role in the camp. Meanwhile—"

Nicoletta tried to cut him off, "*mio caro*. You could not be further—"

Dante raised a palm to stop her. "You know it is true. I see it in your eyes. Without a battle, I am no longer a warrior. I am nothing more than glorified childcare, and I am failing at that too."

Nicoletta rose, the old mattress creaking as she did, to cup Dante's chin in her hands, guiding his face upwards until their eyes met. She kissed him on the forehead, then rested hers against his, "You should have said something earlier."

"And what? Have you create some menial task for me to perform?"

She drew him close.

"I would never trivialise your importance to myself or the camp. Neither would I expect you to do anything beneath you… well, let me rephrase that." She attempted to lighten the atmosphere.

Dante, being Dante, could not help but chuckle at the not-so-subtle innuendo.

"*Amor*, I understand our lives are not as they once were.

Peace was not a state we were taught to appreciate. We were reared by conflict and death but we both know what comes with complacency. Inevitably, mankind will find a way to wage war. So, stay alert, *amante*. Your special talents will be needed before you know it."

"Is that a wish, Nic?"

Her answer, an impish smile.

With the lithe grace of an Olympic figure skater, Dante stood and lifted Nicoletta, his hands spanning her waist.

Managing not to bang his wife's head on the ceiling, he carried her to the bed, which squealed its dissatisfaction at supporting their combined weight, eliciting soft laughter from the couple.

Limbs entwined, the pair shared their first passion-filled kiss in longer than either cared to acknowledge.

Despite the chill of the abandoned inn, and undisturbed by their children, the two rekindled a fire each feared had been extinguished from their relationship.

Until…

"You men, find shelter for the horses while we scout out somewhere to bed down for the night."

Disturbed by the commotion outside, Nicoletta and Dante dressed hurriedly, albeit reluctantly, and crept to the window.

In the courtyard, pulled by a team of six, black Murgese stallions, was an elaborately decorated carriage bearing the

City of Florence coat of arms and the standard of the city's Condottiero Glorioso.

Dante snickered, "Glorious Leader, indeed. Is it not ridiculous how those without genuine strength bestow on themselves such exalted titles?"

Bands of Hunters in the surrounding regions had a history of skirmishes with this man over border disputes, all of which had ended with the condottiero and his minions scurrying back to the north.

Nicoletta jabbed Dante with an elbow to shut him up so she could hear why these city-dwellers dared to enter their lands.

Surrounding the carriage was what appeared to be the remnants of the Florentine House Guard. While they strove to maintain a modicum of security for the occupants of the coach, it was glaringly obvious to the two observing from above that the riders had come out on the losing end of a confrontation.

Under the light of the torches carried by several of the guards, the Hunters saw white uniform jackets liberally stained with blood — presumably, the result of said battle — and splattered with mud. Some of the contingent were slumped over in their saddles, holding onto their lives as tightly as they gripped the reins of their mounts.

"Get the injured indoors now," a rider instructed, nudging his horse close enough to the carriage door to allow it to swing open while protecting those within.

A portly, well-dressed man alighted. He turned to offer a hand to someone inside.

"Come, my love. I know this does not have the opulence of our villa, but we only have to endure it for the night. We will reach Rome soon and you'll be able to rest properly," the man's voice boomed into the night.

A woman could be heard excoriating, "By all that's holy, Luca. How could you think yourself a worthy leader when those barbarians waltzed into our home during our anniversary festival to hound us out of the city."

Attempting to maintain his dignity in front of his soldiers the aforementioned Luca countered, "My dear, Sienna, a house can be replaced… but you… you most certainly could not."

"Bah, you are a coward, and your guard is nothing more than a band of drunkards."

Jabbing her finger at the commander of the guards, she barked, "*Comandante Faccia di Porco*, get off your high horse and find me some decent accommodation, this instant."

The commander glared at the speaker. Being called *Pigface* infuriated him to the point he almost reminded her, she had screamed out far less insulting names when the pair had shared the warmth of her marriage bed.

He swallowed a scathing retort and did as she bade. There would be other days to contend with this bitch.

Using the distraction of the woman's ranting to their advantage, Nicoletta and Dante crept down to the lobby.

Dropping to their knees, they peered through the glass doors. They watched as half the guards broke ranks, presumably to carry out the instructions of the condottiero, or and more likely, those of the woman pulling his strings.

As the remaining cadre circled the couple, Nicoletta studied the wife, judging her to be at least two decades younger than her spouse, and definitely the one who called the shots in their relationship.

Nicoletta chuckled.

Glancing at Dante, she whispered, "Consider yourself blessed, I am only half the pain in the ass that one appears to be."

"Only half?" Dante teased as he drew his sword from its sheath.

Following suit, Nicoletta's response was a crude and unambiguous gesture with her middle finger, wasted given he was crawling away from her to crouch behind the battered reception desk.

The two waited in the darkness listening to the sound of approaching voices. Rusty hinges screeched their announcement of the group's entrance.

"...and I expect a comfortable bed, Luca, even if it means you and your worthless guard are up all night hunting for geese."

"Be reasonable, Sienna, my dear. It is late. The men are exhausted, and we'll be gone by daybreak."

Husband and wife continued to bicker while those of the guard dispatched to seek out a room for the mistress, passed the counter without so much as a glance; too busy escaping the harpy's wrath.

The aforementioned Sienna marched across and pounded her fist on the dusty surface of the check-in desk, as though she expected a smiling concierge to materialise, eager to pander to her every whim.

Her annoyance blinded her to the two Hunters, astonished they had not been discovered, wedged behind it.

Even in her frustration that no one was attending to her needs, Sienna's previous life as a dancer manifested when she pirouetted gracefully to face Luca, preparing to deliver another earful.

Seizing her opportunity, Nicoletta leapt out of her hiding place. Scaling the counter, she grabbed Sienna's shoulder with one hand; the tip of her dagger pressing into the soft flesh of the woman's neck, drawing a bead of blood.

Instinctively, Sienna reached for her throat. The blade bit more deeply, and Nicoletta cautioned, "Unless you wish me to sever your head from your shoulders, I recommend lowering your hand."

The two remaining soldiers surged forwards, swords at the ready, only to have the Condottiero's wife wave them back frantically, her hand trembling.

Luca mustered up his courage and addressed the woman currently using Sienna as a shield.

"You, you, Hunter, release my wife immediately. She has suffered enough terror of late to last ten lifetimes."

Nicoletta transferred her grip from the woman's shoulder to her hair. Fingers snarled through the blonde tresses, she yanked Sienna's head backwards, musing, "I am not sure this doe would be worth the effort of mounting. What do you think, *mí amore?*"

Popping up like an olde-worlde toy, Dante appeared beside his wife, his gladius pointed at the guards, menacingly.

"Hmm… maybe. I doubt there is enough grey matter in that skull to give us any trouble cleaning it. That said, those silly Romans might be prepared to trade supplies for her safe passage."

Since the peace treaty between the Hunters and the City of Rome, the arbitrary practice of collecting heads for wall decorations had come to an end — unless it was won in battle.

Dante and Nicoletta had yet to decide whether a skirmish was on the cards.

Luca tried again, this time employing a more conciliatory tone, “Please, I beg you not to harm her.”

The two Hunters shared a puzzled glance, then Dante snorted, “Have you considered we would be doing you and your men a favour by silencing her permanently? Her grating tones are still ringing in my ears.”

“After everything I have lost already, I could not fathom life without her,” the Condottiero paused as though weighing up his words.

“Perhaps you are right after all, sir. Perhaps death at the ends of your blades would be the most merciful of escapes from this accursed dung heap of a dead planet. It could not be any less desirable than being forced to watch those two strangers being executed by the Bolognese during our feast.”

Nicoletta’s mind whirled, she closed her eyes and willed it not to be so. “What did you just say, *porco*? Strangers… what strangers,” she snapped.

“I have no clue. What part of strangers do you not understand?” Luca shot back with a burst of his old spirit. “Though, by their shabby appearance,” he raked a condescending gaze over Dante and Nicoletta, “I would hazard they belonged to your band of lunatics.”

“Watch your mouth, Dweller,” Nicoletta growled, exposing more of Sienna’s throat to the blade.

The two guards dared to advance, their blades raised to strike the female assailant. In a flash, Dante parried the attack, his gladius making swift work of the warriors’ rapiers.

Even so minor a victory sent excitement coursing through Dante's veins, and his heart swelled at protecting his mate in battle for the first time since the twins' birth. While brief, it was enough to make him feel alive, and consider collecting his trophies.

After all it was an engagement.

Nicoletta recognised the glint in Dante's eyes and shook her head in tacit opposition to what he was contemplating.

She heaved an exasperated breath and offered an olive branch to the Condottiero Glorioso. The suggestion not only startled the Florentine, but also her mate.

"If you pledge to have your men stand down, I will release your woman and perhaps we can discuss a plan of action over a meal, while you enlighten us as to who has taken control of your city."

3

The once bustling dining room played host to a subdued assemblage and, while the Hunters shared their rations with the City Dwellers, they remained on alert, prepared to pounce at the drop of an errant eating utensil.

The city guard were no less distrustful of their dining companions. The slightest shuffle from the Hunters, brought the guards to the ready.

Luca's ability to restrain his men and, more so, his wife, astounded Nicoletta and Dante, who were not crass enough to express their opinion.

At the conclusion of the meal, the commander of the guard dispatched his men to various positions outside the inn to prevent any unwanted advances from the dilapidated buildings encircling their impromptu lodgings.

He elected to remain with his employers, his faith in Luca's decision-making on a par with his lack of trust in their uninvited guests.

Once the five were alone, Nicoletta wiped the residue of Florentine wine from her lips, and addressed the Condottiero Glorioso, "If you have had your fill, perhaps you will regale us with your story?"

Luca frowned, unable to decide whether the woman was being sarcastic but, blessed with little imagination and being a man of his word, ignored it. Settling back in his chair he began his tale.

Florence
Three Days Earlier

"Please, Sienna, enough with the guest list. We have already overtaxed the city for the sake of our anniversary," Luca pleaded, pacing the floor of their bedchamber in the Palazzo Vecchio.

"You are the leader of the city, my sweet." Luca's wife huffed like a spoilt child. "Do please learn to behave like one. These ungrateful sots need to learn their place in this world and how privileged they are to have *our* protection."

On the verge of deteriorating into one of their frequent quarrels, the couple's squabble was stifled when unfamiliar rumbles shook the stained-glass windows in their private chambers.

"What the hell?" Bewildered, Sienna met her husband's troubled gaze.

Luca opened the door and peered along the corridor. No one to be seen. He frowned, that was peculiar in itself. The rumbles grew louder, like an encroaching storm.

"I'll be back," he called over his shoulder and hurried towards the best vantage point of the ancient building.

He struggled up the 223 steps to the top of the Arnolfo Tower as quickly as his legs, and heart, allowed.

Reaching the parapet, panting wildly, and drenched in sweat, he was floored at the sight of Florentines running *en masse* towards the Piazza della Signoria, the huge square beneath where he stood. The rippling movement of people, reminiscent of blood through veins.

Behind the throng, Luca saw puffs of filthy smoke billowing over the iconic terracotta tiled roofs of his beloved city, polluting the pristine sky. The roar of whatever evil belched it growing louder with each passing moment.

From his perch, Luca used a megaphone to order his guards, "Do *not* open the palace doors to the stampede. Direct them to the Piazza de' Pitti where there is more room, and they will be safe."

Not to mention, over the river and out of my way.

While his decision sounded logical to the average person, it was actually based on his dread of facing Sienna's recriminations for letting these people traipse through their home. He could handle the citizenry of Florence. His wife was quite another matter.

Efficiently, the guards herded the panicked rush past the Palazzo Vecchio. Witnessing a few fall to the ground under a barrage of truncheon blows because they chose to ignore instructions was motivation enough for the rest to do as they were told.

As the last of the citizens crossed the Arno River via the Ponte Vecchio, Luca saw the first of the mechanical beasts crawl into the Piazza della Signoria.

It bore the banner of the Bolognese Res Publica.

Luca had maintained his position as the Condottiero Glorioso by avoiding all contact with the other cities which were still populated and steering clear of the Southern Hunters when possible.

Behind the lead vehicle as far as the eye could see, a

hotchpotch of war machines in intimidating numbers, trundled ever closer.

"Ahoy," bellowed a man, sitting on the lip of the hatch.

Paying close attention to the stranger who wore a military uniform and was, apparently, equipped for any sort of conflict, Luca saw him lift a hand to the procession behind him, then reach into the hatch and pull out a white flag, waving it exuberantly.

The newcomer reassured Luca, "We come in peace."

Luca paused his story to take a deep swallow of his wine. Its taste induced a twinge of betrayal and cowardice for fleeing, prompting him to mumble a pledge to reclaim Florence… no matter the cost.

"I do not understand," Nicoletta interjected. "You allowed an army to roll into the heart of your city without the slightest intervention?"

"You do not understand, woman," Luca tried to mitigate the military blunder. "We had spent weeks preparing for the celebration."

Flicking his hand at his wife, Luca defended his actions. "She wanted everything to be perfect."

Staggered by the accusation, Sienna narrowed her eyes. "Do not blame me for your stupidity in leaving the city undefended, old man."

Rubbing his temples, Dante ordered, "Enough. Just get on with your story. I would still like to warm my body with my mate."

Rolling her eyes, Nicoletta jabbed her elbow in his ribs.

The chief guard took up his master's story.

"As the condottiero was making his way down from the

parapet, the Mistress made her presence known, joining the party and…"

"You there," Sienna screeched at the leader of the interlopers, "What are you doing in my city? Are you lost?"

Laughter pealed through the battalion.

"Stop laughing. Did you not hear me?" she said, flapping her hands furiously at the odious machines spewing offensive black clouds. "I say away with you, we have no need for whatever you are peddling."

The man handed his flag to an unseen comrade, and climbed down from his position on the turret, sweeping a theatrical bow in front of Sienna. Gently, he grasped her outstretched hand, to brush a cordial kiss to her knuckles.

"Please forgive my lack of manners, good lady. In the world we now find ourselves, it is rare to encounter such a sophisticated hostess."

He chastised his men for their riotous outburst, "I daresay you rabble could take cues on etiquette from this fine lady."

Spotting a faint pink wash up the woman's pale cheeks, the man allowed himself a satisfied grin.

"Please, allow me to introduce myself, m'lady…"

The more the stranger spoke, the more enthralled Sienna became. He was a breath of fresh air, something her husband had long since lost.

"…I am Monsignor Carlyle Worthington, the Pope of Bologna."

"Pope?" a scathing voice interrupted.

Worthington looked beyond Sienna to see Luca behind his wife. Extracting her hand from the clutches of their uninvited guest, the latter sniped, "I have not heard that antiquated term since the fall of the Roman Church."

Worthington's charm slipped slightly.

"Perhaps, it is time someone revived it to re-establish a religion the masses will flock to observe. Especially when they find *I* am their *one true* saviour.

"We all seek protection, and there is no one better to provide it than yours truly. Now, sir, if you will be kind enough to dispatch your daughter…"

"Hey, watch it. She is my wif—"

"I could not care less if she was a cheap harlot." Worthington shut Luca down. "Send her in to fetch food, water, and wine for myself and my men, before I forget my civility."

"I believe you already have." Luca turned to his chief of security, "Escort these ne'er-do-wells from my grounds."

Worthington took a step towards Luca, all set to express his displeasure at the Florentine's churlishness.

Instinctively, both men's hands curled around the hilts of their swords, bloodshed but a cat's whisker away.

Without a second's thought for her safety, Sienna, palms open in a placatory fashion, intervened to diffuse the tensions, "Luca, please, behave yourself."

Her intercession startled not only her husband, but also Worthington, especially after his initial engagement with the woman.

"Surely we have enough food to share with this gracious visitor and his men."

"You cannot be serious, wife," Luca's protest earned a strong rebuke.

"Do not make us appear boorish, Luca. You are the Condottiero Glorioso, act like it and invite this delegation to dine with us."

Masking his humiliation, Luca straightened his shoulders,

grousing, "Welcome to our humble abode. Please join us for dinner."

Amused at the sight of a man being emasculated by his much younger wife, Worthington flashed a smile at Sienna, and fell into step behind his disgruntled host.

Convinced their esteemed guest was awed by the enormity and opulence of the *Salone dei Cinquecento,* the Hall of the Five Hundred, Sienna played the role of consummate hostess to the max, ensuring wine flowed generously and none of the attendees' plates stayed empty.

As the night progressed, fuelled by copious amounts of Florentine wine, Luca's lips loosened.

Setting down his golden goblet and wiping his face on the back of his hand, he turned to Worthington, slurring, "I repeat my early question. What are your intentions? Why did you chase my citizens from their homes? They posed no threat to you."

Worthington swirled the deep red Chianti Classico — a wine, which, in the previous era, had brought fame and tourists to Tuscany. It splashed over the goblet's rim as he swung his hand towards Luca, his gimlet gaze focused on the leader of the city and his absurd question.

His answer did not get the chance to leave his lips because, right at that moment, two of Worthington's men burst into the hall, dragging a man and a woman. Bloodied and dishevelled, their attire was not that of city dwellers.

"Monsignor," the older guard, with a scraggly beard and weathered face, interrupted. "We found these two surveying the land outside the city. They murdered three of our men during the ensuing fracas to detain them."

"How could you let that happen?" Worthington bellowed, getting to his feet and circling the table. Before the man could justify his actions, his head was bouncing across the floor.

Blood dripped from Worthington's sword as he jabbed it at the younger guard. "And why did you bring them to me?"

The man stuttered, "Th-they are Hunters from the south."

***

Nicoletta bit out, "They had names. Isabel and Enzo to be exact, and they had just celebrated their handfasting."

Her caustic remark fell on deaf ears. The story continued as though she had not spoken.

***

"Th-they may possess useful information."

Worthington rebuked, "You made two grave mistakes, lad. The first was thinking for yourself. That is *my* responsibility.

"Second, to believe these two," his upper lip curled contemptuously, "are of *any* worth, especially after allowing themselves to be taken alive, let alone at all…"

Without warning, Worthington stepped between the prisoners and, with a vicious swing of his weapon, decapitated the male. "…just confirms how useless they are."

He sent the female a vicious grin. "What of you, wench? Will you answer my questions in return for your freedom, or shall I turn you over to my men to be used as breeding stock?"

Witness to the death of her mate, the Hunter's eyes narrowed at Worthington in hatred. Despite her wrists being bound behind her back, she lunged at him, impaling herself on his sword.

Worthington jammed his boot into her chest to rid his blade of her before her deadweight could damage it.

Wiping the blood-smeared sword on the woman's tunic, Worthington faced the table where his host and hostess sat in slack-jawed stupefaction.

"I declare this celebration concluded, as well as your leadership of this city."

Luca bounded to his feet. "How dare you? You are in no position to usurp my authority."

"Quite the contrary you obese blowhard. As anyone possessing an ounce of wit would have guessed by now, your city is encircled by my forces and cut off from the rest of the world.

"By my divine right, I shall cleanse this Godforsaken peninsula of your kind by completing the task Mother Nature was unable to accomplish. Only the strong will be left to inherit this contaminated rock."

Worthington took one stride towards the table, to be blocked by the city guard.

The security chief warned, "Not one step closer."

"Or what?" Worthington sneered, electing to speak with his blade rather than wait for a response.

The deafening clang of steel against steel reverberated around the hall. Hands grasped the back of the Condottiero Glorioso's tunic, urging him, and his wife past the ancient statuary and murals adorning the Hall… the beautiful and priceless artworks being liberally splattered with blood… to the stone staircase beyond an innocuous doorway at the end of the room.

Finally shocked into silence, Sienna did not argue or protest at being roughly handled. Sheet white, she ran alongside her husband.

Bundled through the door, the pair hurried up the steps, heading for the, now very shabby, Hall of the Maps, and an escape route known to a handful of Luca's most trusted men, all of whom were alongside the couple.

The Vasari Corridor.

Connected to the Uffizi Gallery by an enclosed overpass at the south side of the Palazzo Vecchio, the corridor was commissioned by Cosimo de' Medici as a way to move freely and safely between his two palaces.

Slipping behind the map of Armenia, Luca waited until everyone had followed him through the gap, then let the painting swing back into place.

Along with the palace, the Uffizi and its hidden walkway was left derelict after the global catastrophe. Luca, who happened to appreciate and was rather knowledgeable about art, had spent an enormous amount of energy protecting and restoring the collection, now displayed along the length of the corridor.

Scurrying along in the flickering flame of a single torch, Luca mourned the fact this might be the last time he would see his precious paintings, quashing the notion the figures depicted, illuminated eerily by the rising moon, were mocking him for abandoning them in the same ignoble manner as had his predecessors.

No time for introspection, the fleeing party skirted the River Arno, following the same route the citizenry had taken earlier in the day, although *this* path conveyed them above the Lungarno degli Archibusieri.

Their trek took them over the Ponte Vecchio — aging witness to the rise of Florence, and the only bridge spared destruction in the last 'world' war, allegedly, because the installation of the larger windows in the centre by a former Italian dictator had provided *his* megalomaniac overlord with a panoramic view.

The irony of that was not lost on Luca.

They sped across the loggiato of the church of Santa Felicita, then under numerous connected roofs, emerging at the Palazzo Pitti where the Condottiero Glorioso's carriage stood in a perpetual state of readiness on the off chance a situation of this nature arose.

Luca and Sienna climbed aboard, and the company set off with all haste to the southern gates of the city, hoping to avoid any of Worthington's men.

Unfortunately, Luck was still vacillating over whose side she was on.

While only a small contingent of the monsignor's soldiers policed the road leading to the countryside, they were deadly enough to cut through Luca's forces before being overwhelmed by the sheer numbers of the city guard.

At full gallop, the entourage escaped into the night but not before Luca, hearing a thunderous explosion and an ominous clanging, glanced out of the window at the back of the carriage.

The night sky lit up in the fireball caused by a projectile striking the centuries old campanile adjacent to the Duomo.

Luca closed his eyes, mourning the loss of the ancient tower and hoped the huge bell landed on some of the thugs underneath — in his mind, a fair trade for obliterating so beautiful a monument.

He concluded, "We raced at breakneck speed until we crossed into your lands."

"Did you expect us to offer sanctuary?" Dante scoffed.

Luca shook his head. "No, but we have heard of your

treaty with Rome and hoped your leader would grant us safe passage to the city."

With a weary sigh, he added, "Even if she does not, I surmise death at your hands will be more expeditious and less gruesome than at those of the Bolognese."

Dante snorted, "Then you best pray to whichever deity you worship, our padrona is in a good mood when you meet her."

"And when might that be?" Sienna chimed in.

"Have your men free up two of their horses. My woman and I will be needing them," Dante replied. "We leave in the morning, and neither myself nor my mate plan to walk."

4

The entourage made good progress on the first day but, the following evening, the weather broke, and an overnight downpour gave way to a cold, miserable, steady rain.

The unceasing deluge caused the numerous potholes in the sadly neglected Via Braccianese Claudia to fill with water, concealing their depths.

While those on horseback were able to avoid them, regrettably, the carriage could not. The wooden wheels buried themselves into the deep ruts, resulting in the vehicle jolting precariously, threatening to overturn it completely, and provoking a volley of curses.

"Dammit, man, we want to arrive at their encampment in one piece… not twenty," Luca castigated the coachman testily, for the umpteenth time.

By mid-morning, the carriage could take the abuse no longer. As the right wheel slewed into a particularly deep furrow, it separated from the axle, spun wildly down an embankment and into a gulley. The axle dropped sharply, and gouged the deteriorating tarmac, causing the conveyance to lurch drunkenly.

The shaft snapped, releasing the six horses, and the abrupt shift in weight sent the white coach skidding on its side along the thoroughfare.

One of the guards, compelled to surrender his mount to the Hunters, was tossed out of the carriage, to be crushed when it landed on him.

The coachman fared no better. Unable to loosen his grip on the reins, he was yanked from his seat and dragged to his death by the thundering steeds.

The guards were quick to halt their advance to survey and triage the surviving occupants of the mangled carriage, while the two Hunters, seemingly unaware of the catastrophe unfolding behind them, had to be chased down some two miles further along the muddy road.

Under armed escort, Dante and Nicolette were herded back to the site of the accident, where they overheard Sienna complaining of severe pain radiating from her right shoulder. The company lacked their field medic who was killed in the skirmish at the city gates.

With no other trained medical personnel, the commander of the guard was forced to rely on the very people who undoubtedly intended to abandon the group at the first opportunity… like right now.

Galled at being reduced to begging, the commander swallowed hard, tempering his frustration. "The mistress is injured and the Condottiero Glorioso is unconscious and unresponsive. Please attend to them."

Nicoletta and Dante exchanged irritated glances. Both would prefer to continue galloping for camp; but were concerned with Sophia's reaction if she were to discover their decision led to the untimely death of these idiot city dwellers.

Dismounting, Nicoletta brushed past the man, who was attempting and failing to pacify Sienna, growling at him, "Unless your aim is to incapacitate her, step aside."

The commander, about to engage in a war of words with the female Hunter, swallowed his wrath when Sienna wailed, "Please, let her do her job."

Nicoletta winced at the description of the skill she had taken years to achieve first under Bianca's and then Sophia's tutelage summed up as a *job*.

Determining Sienna was suffering from a dislocated collarbone, Nicoletta barked an order to the commander, "Get behind her and brace her."

Grasping Sienna close to her clavicle, she warned the woman, "This is gonna…"

Maybe applying a little too much pressure in the process, Nicoletta performed a closed reduction procedure, realigning Sienna's collarbone. The Florentine's scream drowned the conclusion of Nicoletta's warning that it would, "…hurt like hell."

Succumbing to the acute agony, Sienna passed out, which suited Nicoletta perfectly. She had no desire to hear anymore squawking from this bird.

She bound Sienna's arm against her body to ensure it was immobilised, then joined Dante who, with the aid of the guards, was extricating Luca from the wreckage of the carriage.

A length of splintered wood had pierced Luca's thigh. Noting its position, Nicoletta surmised it had severed his femoral artery.

Her yelled, "Don't pull it out," came too late. One of the guards took it upon himself to do just that. Blood arced from the punctured limb, spraying those around Luca.

"Put his ass down," Dante ordered, yanking off his belt. Although not in his nature to save a life, attested to by the display of trophy heads on their wall, when his mate put her training into practice, his response was instinctive.

Tying a tourniquet above the gaping wound, Dante cinched the belt, fighting to stem the vivid red fountain, murmuring for Nicoletta's ears only, "Bunch of horses' asses this lot. I am guessing from the amount of blood this over-stuffed bugger is losing, he is not long for this world."

Nicoletta shook her head, replying in kind, "Even if I had my sewing kit, which I am sure, I told *you* to put in my pack, or a blazing fire burning so we can cauterise the wound, I doubt it would do any good. Never a highly skilled sawbones, full surgical team, and clean instruments around when you need them..." she left that dangling. "Do you have any brilliant ideas?"

"Give him a nice funeral pyre?" Dante flashed the briefest of smirks to his mate, who swallowed an irreverent chortle.

Damn the man, she thought to herself, *no matter the situation, he still finds the stupidest ways to make me laugh.*

With an eye to the guards encircling them, he added, "We might have to set the whole place on fire. Pretty sure these guys are gonna pin his imminent demise on us."

As though to emphasise the dilemma they now faced, a rattling gasp for a final breath marked the end of the Condottiero Glorioso's reign of Florence... and his life.

Nicoletta and Dante looked at the man's lips which began to take on a bluish tinge.

Nicoletta hissed, "Fuck." while Dante's brain went off on a tangent.

"Can I keep his head? As a souvenir of course."

"Dammit, husband, how many times do I have to repeat the rules? Only if it is a war trophy. If anyone deserves it, it would be the worthless coachman who could not avoid a pothole. Besides, you know Sophia has started to frown on the practice."

"Yeah, only because she can't go hunting any more. Piss poor excuse if you ask me."

"Hush," Nicoletta instructed *sotto voce,* nodding at the man who, until a split second ago, was the head of the Condottiero Glorioso's security detail. "You'll still end up with one or two."

Said chief demanded, "You there, what is his status?"

Getting to her feet, Nicoletta side-stepped her husband, brushing her hands together, allowing Dante to rise behind her and ready his sword for battle.

"Let's just say, he will not have to be concerned with the Bolognese advancing anymore," her reply was devoid of inflection.

"What?"

"He is dead, you dimwit," Dante enunciated each word with deliberation.

The guard shrieked, "You killed him."

Swords rattled as he and his men swarmed around the Hunters.

"Hardly, that lunkhead over there…" Nicoletta waved a dismissive hand at the guard who had wrenched the wooden spike from Luca's thigh. "…might as well have taken his blade and cleaved your padrone's head from his shoulders."

"Do not blame my men for your inadequacies," the commander retorted, drawing his sword from its scabbard. "I know all too well you planned to murder him from the moment our paths crossed."

"Are you insane?" Nicoletta refuted, whipping out her own blade. "If that was the case, your heads would be in our packs already, destined for our wall."

The Hunters spun back-to-back in a defensive stance, while the guards closed in on them.

Before steel could announce the approach of Death… *again…* a voice bellowed above the din, "Enough, all of you."

The bristling adversaries swivelled to face its source.

Hobbling painfully, Sienna made her way to the corpse of her former husband. Kneeling next to Luca, she brushed a light caress to his battered face. As much as she had profited from Luca's position, she realised too late... and after too many affairs... she had loved him in her own warped way.

Left with a guilt, from which she could never rid herself, tears brimmed over to spill down her cheeks. Studiously avoiding eye contact with the commander of the guard, she directed her remarks at the Hunters, "Has there not been enough needless destruction in the last few days without feeding the beast all the more?"

"Your men drew *first*, woman," Dante countered. "Do not expect us to stand here like lemons and wait for them to slice us up."

"Commander. Tell the guard to sheathe their weapons," Sienna ordered, holding his gaze until he signalled his men to comply.

"There, sir. Are you satisfied?"

Nicoletta and Dante traded uncertain glances.

"Please, I beseech you," Sienna implored. "My husband has lost his life through no fault of his own. May we maintain the peace he brokered, and continue on to meet with your leader?"

"What of your deceased mate?" Dante inquired curiously. "What do you intend to do with his body?"

"Is there any way to take him with us? I should hate him to become fodder for wild animals. He deserves a better send off than that."

"We could always honour him with our custom," Nicoletta offered, reminiscing on Dante's prior suggestion.

"Set him on fire? How barbaric," Sienna let slip without considering how her words might upset the Hunters.

Catching herself, she tried to placate, "Our customs are

akin to those practiced in Rome. If we can get his body there, I am sure they would see to his internment."

Too late.

Nicoletta's reply was unyielding, "To our camp and no further. If it was up to me, I would rather see his bones wither under the sun, but that decision lies with my padrona. For now, have your men build a sledge and attach it to one of your horses. Whether you walk, or ride is your responsibility. Whatever your choice, make it quick, we cannot tarry."

It took Sienna's men the rest of the morning to fell and strip enough trees to construct a sledge sturdy enough to convey Luca's body, and another hour to lash everything together.

Fortunately for all, the cool air had, so far, inhibited Nature's determination to claim the remains of their illustrious Condottiero Glorioso.

Once they were set, the commander assisted Sienna onto his horse. Silently, she wrapped her good arm around his waist and laid her head against his back.

Gently spurring on his mount, the commander fell in line with the rest of the entourage, taking up position behind Luca's funeral procession.

Silence hung over the riders for the last leg of the journey. The drum of hooves and the grinding of wood against the road was the only resonance to break it.

The following day, under the soft purple sky of the gathering dusk, the glaring lights from the camp came into view.

Dante and Nicoletta experienced a wave of relief at the welcome sight of Antonio and Angelo approaching across the plains with a brigade of men but hid it well; neither brother needed their egos stroking.

"Hold up there," Angelo commanded. "If you think bringing these two to us as an exchange for passage, you had best think twice. They are well aware what their capture by the likes of you means."

It was Dante who put an end to the chest pounding.

"Enough of your sabre rattling, Angelo. Shut your mouth and fetch your mate. The padrona's presence is needed."

Piqued that his rank as Sophia's man was not being respected by either Nicoletta or Dante, Angelo retorted, "Any decisions to be made concerning this motley crew you have dragged into camp is well within my prerogative."

Nicoletta sighed, "Just go fetch Sophia, so we can stop worrying about when this corpse is going to ripen and burst open."

5

“Angelo, I gave you one task…” Sophia chastised her mate all the way to the clearing. “…watch the perimeters while Nicoletta is gone and do not kill anything.

“How do you and that feckless brother of yours go from defence to offence not only against a whole other faction of dwellers… but also my head of security in the blink of an eye? Are you *trying* to induce premature labour?”

Exasperated, she threw up her hands, as Bianca chimed in, “If you succeed, I shall take great delight in gutting you.”

About to justify his actions, Angelo’s attention was caught by the dark, bulky shape heading their way at speed.

The squeal of laughter from the three smaller creatures, easily outdistancing their pursuer left Angelo in no doubt as to the identities.

The booming voice of Gabriel brought Bianca and Sophia to a standstill, and the pair swung around to observe the failure in childcare.

“Dammit, Aurora, enough!”

Giggling hysterically, Aurora taunted, "Can't catch me, Papa."

Angelo readied himself to corral the twins, if for no other reason than to prove he was a better babysitter than Gabriel.

Rocco and Zara were having none of it.

Nicoletta and Dante's wild offspring avoided capture by splitting off right and left, leaving Angelo to face plant into the clump of grass as he tried to intercept them.

Gabriel scooped up his daughter with a "*Gotcha,*" as she closed in on her mother and aunt. In one fluid motion, he flipped her onto his shoulders.

Spotting their parents, and ignoring Sophia's exhortations that their shrieks would raise the dead, the twins bounced in excitement. "Mama... Papa."

Raised around horses, Rocco and Zara knew better than to advance too quickly which could spook the mounts. Slowing several feet away, they stopped whooping, and walked calmly to Nicoletta's grey mare, stretching out for her to pull them up.

Gabriel joined Bianca, who shook her head at her mate in disbelief that he was outwitted by a trio of children.

Shrugging his massive shoulders, jostling his daughter in the process, he defended himself with a muttered, "Don't blame me, they carry the Hunters' genes after all."

On tiptoes, Bianca brushed a loving kiss to Gabriel's cheek. "Looks like you may need more childcare lessons, my love."

"Not my fault," Gabriel reiterated. "It was three against one, and I swear those two..." he flicked a hand in the direction of Rocco and Zara, "...are evil incarnate."

"Hey, now. Watch your words, *Farmer,*" Nicoletta shot back, using a nickname the Hunters had bestowed on Gabriel during the early days. "These are *my* little darlings, and if anyone is going to accuse them of being in league with the underworld it shall be me."

Rocco giggled, "You should have seen Uncle Gabriel's face when he tripped over the stri—"

Nicoletta nudged her son who took one look at his mother and buttoned his lips.

Disregarding the whole parental disagreement, Sophia greeted Nicoletta, "Did you learn anything of value in the north, or did you simply collect the riff-raff along the way?"

"I beg your pardon, whatever your name is..." Sienna interjected.

"To you, it is Padrona, and you best curb your tongue before it is removed. I am addressing my security chief." Sophia shot Sienna a flinty glare.

"I apologise for her," Nicoletta lamented. "I've been trying to silence her since we crossed paths... to no avail."

"Did you try a gag?" Bianca proposed.

"Keeping your mouth shut goes for you too, or I'll gag you instead," Sophia rebuked her sister.

"Pregnancy has certainly made you grouchy."

Dismissing Bianca's comment, Sophia repeated, "Who are these people and why have you allowed them to trespass onto our lands?"

Nicoletta gave her leader a succinct account of the events which had occurred at the boundary lands... glossing over the fact, Dante and she lacked the expertise to save Luca's life, then indicated the sledge trussed up to the weary horse.

"I knew you would frown on us leaving him to the wolves."

For the first time in her life, Nicoletta had misjudged Sophia who chided, "So you brought him here, not knowing what diseases he might harbour."

Aggrieved, Sienna countered, "I can assure you the

Condottiero Glorioso of Florence carried no diseases, save maybe an oversized heart for his people."

The commander, to whom she still clung, could not believe his ears. Many were the nights she had complained of Luca's neglect, yet here she was extolling the lout's virtues.

He considered dumping Sienna's ass on the soggy ground but chalked up her sudden and belated marital bliss to the shock of losing her husband.

Anything we need to hash out can wait until a less... fraught time.

It was Bianca who spoke for the health of the camp, "We couldn't care less if you believe your man was a snow-white virgin, but there's no saying he wasn't infected with any number of viruses prior to his death. Dante." Bianca turned her attention to Nicoletta's mate. "Swap mounts with that soldier and drag the sorry corpse around the outskirts of the camp to the back of my wagon where we will prepare for his disposal."

"Please," for the second time in eighteen hours, Sienna begged for the preservation of Luca's remains. "All we ask is that you permit us to cross your lands in order to take my husband to Rome for a proper burial."

Sophia attempted to clarify, "If you do not allow us to prepare his body for your onward journey, you will have nothing left for interment; but if that is your choice—"

"N-No." Catching Sophia's expression, Sienna backpedalled. "Please, do what you can, and thank you."

"Nicoletta, while Bianca and I attend to your mess, take *your guests* to the southern trail and let them set up camp. As for their new Padrona, make her comfortable in the caravan next to mine."

"Yes, Padrona — wait, that is ours."

"Your mess, your problem," Sophia justified with an unrepentant wink.

At the edge of the encampment, in a caravan specifically assigned… and thus avoided like the plague by everyone else… for all things medical, and employing the skills their mother taught them, Sophia and Bianca worked as diligently as had the ancient barber-surgeons of the Middle Ages.

Washing Luca's body prior to eviscerating him, Bianca protested, "Would it not be easier to use formaldehyde as Mama described in the before-times, instead of this painstaking procedure?"

"I am sure it would. Do you have a couple of litres on you?"

Bianca grimaced. "Top shelf back at my place."

"Not much good there." Sophia shook her head. "Get busy and open him up."

Even though Bianca was the elder of the two, she allowed her sister to throw her weight around. Preferring to spend time with her husband and child, as well as immersing herself in her mother's assorted and numerous textbooks on everything health-related, Bianca had relinquished leadership of the camp to Sophia. A choice she never regretted… except when Sophia got bossy.

That… and the fact Sophia was almost due… were all that stood between her adored younger sister and a well-deserved trouncing.

Adhering to the instructions Noemi had drilled into her daughters, Bianca cut a Y-shaped incision from Luca's shoulders to his sternum, then down to his pelvis.

Aware the majority of the man's blood had soaked the verge of the Via Braccianese Claudia, she was unmoved by the lack thereof in the cadaver, which had settled to his posterior; she had seen too much death.

Sophia mixed the disinfecting fluids they would need to cleanse the body cavity once the organs were removed. Despite its intended use, the medicinal concoction emitted a heady aroma of spices and herbs.

Finished gutting the Florentine Condottiero Glorioso, Bianca placed his organs in jars containing a watered down version of the mixture Sophia had concocted, and set them on an adjacent bench.

In the past, honouring the rites of other tribes, especially traditional burial practices implemented by the city dwellers was outside the Hunters' consideration.

Times had changed and, to avoid a repeat of the recent hostilities, the Roman ruler, Callixtus, seized every opportunity to assimilate the various customs among his allies, as part of his determination to forge a lasting peace between the Hunters and Dwellers.

That the Padrona of the Hunters was performing this ritual, strengthened the fragile bonds, and demonstrated their burgeoning mutual respect, particularly given the identity of the recipient.

Coating the chest cavity in the gelatinous ointment, the pair filled the corpse with thyme, rosemary, and lavender to ensure the putrid odour of decaying flesh would be minimised until they reached the walled city.

Bianca closed the incision neatly, then the two women covered him in layers of cerecloth — the waxed bindings used for this purpose — and sealed the seams with beeswax.

Here their involvement ended, for to venerate Luca further was beyond their purview. The Hunters' homage to their revered dead was a pyre.

Who had the wherewithal to tote the heavy, ornate coffins the Dwellers deemed essential for miles in order to ensure their dead could be conveyed to whichever afterlife they believed in from an 'approved' basilica?

The pair stretched a tarpaulin over the body to protect it from the elements.

"I hope Callixtus does not hold us responsible for this man's demise," Bianca muttered as they secured the body to the bed of the wagon.

"Doubtful," Sophia reassured. "The man's head is still attached to his shoulders."

Bianca could not help but chuckle at her sister's flippant assessment.

"If he does, I'll send Dario to deal with him."

"Dario? Dante's brother? Do tell, what I have been missing here?"

"Hmmm... you haven't missed anything... yet." Sophia winked impishly. "Let us just say that Callixtus has been instrumental in helping Dario surmount his grief at Rolando's death during the raid of the Roman armoury, and Dario is strengthening our ties with Rome."

"Is that a convoluted way of saying they are an item?" Bianca asked in amusement.

"I am not one for spreading rumours," Sophia smirked.

Knowing her sister better than that, Bianca rolled her eyes. When they were children, their mother could get Sophia to spill any secret Bianca had entrusted to her sibling, simply by bribing her with a cookie.

"Now that this one is unlikely to wander off, I think we ought to visit your guest to ensure she is comfortable."

"I suppose you're right," Sophia agreed. "Will you and Gabriel be joining us on the trip to Rome in the morning?"

"If I expect to get my donkey and cart back, I have no choice. Besides, I can use the chance to replenish my supplies and check on my students there. That said, I shall leave you to inform my beloved husband of the trip."

"I will make sure he is wined and dined before I do."

They giggled like two schoolgirls as they trudged across the camp to Nicoletta's caravan.

6

A sudden and vigorous pounding on Sophia's caravan door jolted the occupants awake.

Aurora, who had overheard the adults discussing the terrible creatures of the north, imagined they had found their way to the camp, and gave vent to a scream worthy of a banshee.

Ignoring the unceasing racket at the front door, Bianca and Gabriel hurried to comfort their daughter.

Sophia was not as focused.

The battering at the door had startled her baby, who gave a forceful jerk inside Sophia's womb, making that young lady yelp and curse up a storm at Angelo for whatever he was doing.

She grumbled, "No doubt the lummox is in the kitchen destroying it with one of his midnight snacks."

Belatedly, when the noise failed to dissipate, she remembered she had assigned her mate and his brother to watch over the Florentines on the southern path, meaning it was up to her to mete out justice. The padrona swore merciless retribution on whoever dared disturb her and her unborn child.

Marching across the bedroom to deal with the intruder at the door, she was about to grab her daggers from the dressing table, only to recall that Nicoletta had removed and destroyed them because they were old and dull.

Opening her closet, Sophia dug through the clutter seeking anything deadly enough to confront the cause of the commotion. Her outrage morphed into a wicked grin when she came across her father's ancient claymore, a weapon nearly as large as she.

Sophia swung the massive blade, ready to lop the head off the plague-sore at the other side of the door but, in her muddled, anger-fuelled haze, forgot the height limitation of the caravan, and the claymore slammed against the ceiling with a resounding thud. Violent shockwaves shuddered down the sword, and it took sheer effort of will, not to drop it.

Tightening her grip, Sophia charged to the door, skidding to a stunned halt and rendered speechless when she came face-to-face with Gabriel.

Since the day Noemi had gifted him the military blade, once the proud possession of Bianca and Sophia's father, Gabriel had assumed the role of protector. Prepared to defend the sisters with his life, his dark eyes glinted dangerously as he waited for Sophia to give him the signal to pounce on the interloper.

Secretly, Sophia was impressed by the farmer's bold stance. *Not* that she was about to apprise him of this.

I wish I *had found you before Bianca did,* she thought, giving him a nod.

Grasping the knob, Gabriel yanked open the door, nearly wrenching it from its hinges. Blades slashed into the darkness, to be met by a horrified scream.

"What in Hades?" Sienna shrieked as she leapt off the steps to avoid being bisected. "Is that how you welcome all your guests?"

There was a clatter inside the caravan as weapons were put aside.

"It is not customary that we entertain guests at all, especially before the sun rises." Sophia retorted.

"Did you not tell me last night we would depart at first light? My men are ready…" Sienna looked the pair up and down, "…why are you not?"

Caught by her own instructions, Sophia swore under her breath and conceded, with bad grace, "Sometimes. I'm too well-organised for my own good. I did not expect you to take that literally. It was simply a warning not to lie abed 'til midday."

For the first time since Worthington invaded her city Sienna felt a grin emerging. Determining… correctly as it happened… that a facetious response *not* be well-received, she pressed her lips together, and, as primly as possible, apologised for her misunderstanding.

Exasperated as she was Sophia, spotting the twitch of the woman's lips, felt a chuckle of her own threatening. All she said, however, was, "Well played, don't make a habit of it."

The sun had barely breached the distant horizon when the Hunters set off for Rome.

Grasping the donkey's harness, Gabriel guided the cart onto the trail leading south.

The women were afforded the relative comfort of the cart's narrow, wooden bench seat; flanked by Sophia's security squad.

The children remained at the camp under the watchful eyes of the nannies. Their respective parents had determined exposing them to a lifestyle the Hunters still deemed overly ostentatious, and perhaps somewhat lacking in the discipline department, would be confusing for ones so young, and almost certainly prompt a score of awkward questions better answered another day.

Silently, Sienna's guards trudged behind the cortège.

The herbs and spices with which Sophia and Bianca had laced the corpse, succeeded in masking the stench of death, although a hint lingered, reminding them that time was not on their side.

By noon, the entourage had reached Gabriel and Bianca's cottage. Bianca thought it wise to take a break there. The jostling of the cart had left Sophia feeling more irritable than Sienna's intrusion of her caravan.

Bianca's training prompted her to conduct a swift examination of her sister to ensure the bouncing of the wagon had not triggered Sophia's labour.

Fortunately, it had not but, concerned, Bianca felt moved to ask, "Are you sure you do not want to spend the rest of the day here? You are in no shape to complete the journey."

"Are you serious, and let Callixtus believe I am unfit to hold my position as padrona?"

"Sophia you are in your last month of pregnancy. I am sure he would understand your absence considering your conditi—"

"Oh come on, I reckon that would give Callixtus more reason to see me as some fragile female—"

"...a heavily encumbered one," Bianca countered mildly.

"Which would be even worse; and please don't tell me you expected Angelo to handle this delicate delegation?"

To the surprise of both women, Bianca championed Sophia's mate. Even though Bianca had spent the better part of her life tormenting the brothers, she felt, at times, Sophia did not give Angelo the credit he deserved.

"He cannot be a total moron if you chose to have a child with him."

"Well, not everyone is as lucky as you, are they?"

The outburst silenced Bianca who blanched at her sister's insinuation.

As the words fell from her lips, Sophia realised what she had said, hectic colour flaring up her cheeks. Professing to be jealous of her sister's relationship with Gabriel was not, never had been, her intention, but she couldn't help it, cursing herself inwardly for the slip.

Without a word, Bianca turned on her heel and headed to the stable, leaving her sister stumbling for an apology. She returned a short time later astride her pony, Belle, the one Sophia had gifted her after their escape from Rome.

"Bianca, I did not mean anything—"

"Time to go," was all Bianca replied, her face closed.

Sophia climbed up onto the hard wooden bench seat, chewing over how she could make Bianca understand that she did not want Gabriel, *per se,* she just wanted Angelo to be a bit more like him.

She had spent so many years perfecting the art of independence that her, for want of a better word, mate had no clue how to behave around her. Of late, their conversations tended to deteriorate into sarcasm and sly digs; neither seemed capable of breaking the habit of a lifetime.

Even Sophia's pregnancy had not softened their caustic exchanges, although, to be scrupulously fair… if she really had to be… so far, Angelo had made far more of an effort than she.

Her expression turned glum.

In truth, the poor bugger was a glutton for punishment; he was the one who had done all the compromising. She had argued that her role as padrona came first; everything else was of secondary importance.

Am I mistaken? The very fact she had posed the question gave her the answer.

A frown formed as, absently, her hand stroked over the aged wood of the cart's frame, and a series of images chased through her head. That awful moment in Settebagni when she thought he had been killed, or worse, taken captive. The succeeding months when something more tangible had kindled between them.

What happened, Angelo? she sent the question to the skies. *You took him for granted,* a very annoying voice at the back of her head – which sounded suspiciously like Noemi, or possibly even Bianca, given her recent defence of Angelo – reminded, *and rather than bring down your wrath on his head for any number of slights imagined or otherwise, he avoids confrontation, which creates a distance... one you refuse to cross.*

Lost in thought, she was scarcely aware the wagon had lurched forwards, nor did she hear the steady rumble of the wheels on the dry track. Much as she disliked fighting with her sister, Bianca's reaction had brought her relationship with her mate into sharp focus.

It was time she was honest with herself and Angelo. There was no doubt theirs was more than a passing affection. The idea of him abandoning her for another woman made Sophia's heart ache... not that she was about to enlighten him of this... and thereby hung the problem.

What had Noemi always said? Her mother's voice echoed in her mind, "Communication is key. Without it you might as well try to fly with a cannon ball tied to your ankles."

A peculiar analogy, but one easily understood by two flighty young girls who presumed they did not have to explain themselves to anyone... ever.

Huffing an aggrieved sigh, Sophia acknowledged she had

at least two bridges to mend. She hated admitting she was wrong. Mind… one smug remark and she was outta there… they could swing, the lot of them.

7

The walls of Rome loomed on the horizon. Bianca encouraged Belle into a canter, putting a sizeable distance between herself and the funeral party.

Stopping long enough to present her identification card at the gate and, jokingly, promising the guard not to cause any unnecessary death and destruction, Bianca headed to the house, nestled in the Garbetella neighbourhood.

She was keenly aware, even with Gabriel and Sophia's presence, it would take a personal appearance from Callixtus to grant access to the Florentines.

This gave Bianca more than enough time to reach their city abode, make sure it was presentable... even for her damnable sister... and savour some of her husband's cherished wine to brighten her mood.

In exchange for Bianca providing medical education to the city's population, and in apology for the atrocities the previous Tribunal had inflicted on Gabriel and Bianca, one of Callixtus' first decrees as Rome's Chancellor was to reinstate the couple's ownership of this house and their vineyards outside the walls.

Bianca missed the taste of her farmer's wine, but Gabriel had leased the lands to some locals for their own use. Tending the vines had become uneconomical, being too far from their cottage, and neither parent wanted to raise their daughter in the city.

The couple could not come to an agreement as to whether to sell the property. Currently, except for their infrequent trips to Rome, it sat vacant.

Gabriel had hired Minerva and her daughter, their erstwhile next-door neighbours, to keep an eye on the house, overseeing its maintenance and arranging any necessary repairs.

Dismounting, Bianca led Belle along the narrow passage between the houses to the rear courtyard, tethering the pony to the post adjacent to the water trough, so she might quench her thirst.

Patting Belle's flank, Bianca retraced her steps to the front door, taking a moment to admire the façade, generously restored by Minerva's husband, Pietro, aware Gabriel would compensate their kindly neighbours for their efforts.

Unlocking the huge wooden door, she reacquainted herself with the house, smiling when she was greeted by an immaculately clean kitchen.

Large amphorae storing various blends of wine were propped against the far wall, and two bottles of Gabriel's Chianti from the last harvest before his decision to sublet the vineyards, sat on the kitchen counter, waiting to be opened.

Bianca was not one to refuse the command of a full-bodied red.

Uncorking the bottle, she grinned at the cheerful *pop*, and poured herself a decent glass. The first sip did not fail to bring relief from the anguish of the day.

The dryness of the wine spoke of the qualities of the Sangiovese grapes which gave it life. She particularly enjoyed the drink's ease of consumption, conscious she had already imbibed half the measure.

Swirling the Chianti as she climbed the stairs, she noticed a cloth covering their dining table, confident it was highly polished and ready for use.

Her next stop was the second-floor great room.

Bianca was impressed to see everything covered in more clean sheets. That Minerva was fastidious enough to ensure the sheets protecting the furniture underneath from dust were swapped regularly, was a balm to Bianca's perfectionism.

"Well, that is one less chore I have to contend with," Bianca said to the empty room, in relief.

Ascending to the top floor, and the bed chambers, Bianca set her glass on the nightstand and sat on the edge of the bed.

She considered stretching out and taking a brief nap, but the thunder of hooves put paid to that.

A woman's anguished cry propelled Bianca to the front window in time to witness Gabriel and Dante helping Sophia down from the cart.

Hearing Gabriel bellow to Callixtus to fetch one of his midwives, Bianca surmised her sister's water had broken and she was in labour.

Bianca swung the window wide and shouted to the chancellor, "Do not dare," then to her husband, "Bring her up to our quarters."

Gabriel scooped his sister-in-law into his arms and rushed up the three flights of stairs. By the time he had reached Bianca, she had already stripped the blankets from the bed, and was in one of the other rooms fetching the tinctures and potions she used during a delivery.

Hearing Gabriel's boot thud to a stop at the top of the staircase, she called out, "Put her on our bed, and have Nic join me, I am going to need her help."

"Is there anything you need me to do, mí amore?"

"Yes. Boil some water, grab some rags, and then keep out of my way."

Settling Sofia in their bed, Gabriel looped one arm around his wife as she entered the room. He pulled her close, whispering into her ear, "Sophia is worried about you. She told me what she had said to you, while I carried her in. You know she meant nothing by that comment. Regardless of which, I have only ever had eyes for you."

The ride from their cottage had given Bianca the clarity to accept the validity of Gabriel's statement. She knew no woman could ever come between them, even if it was Sophia.

She blushed at her girlish pang of jealousy.

Sophia's agonised groan snapped Bianca back to the here and now.

Pressing a kiss to her husband's cheek, she spun him about and swatted him out of the room, reminding him, "Get that cute butt in gear and do what I tell you."

As Gabriel was leaving, Bianca added, "And dispatch someone back to camp to bring Angelo here. The boy needs to be with his mate when the child comes."

Sienna and her men had followed Callixtus to a suite of apartments in the Vatican. He assured his guest, her husband would be moved to the vaults and prepared for his interment.

When it came to acknowledging Bianca's rejection of help from his midwives, Callixtus consented to their dismissal… save one… a woman called Julia.

Julia had spent almost two months under Bianca's tutelage at the latter's cottage, where she had acquired the expertise to ensure a smooth and, usually, straightforward birth.

Bianca met her at the door, but before she could lodge a complaint at the midwife's presence, Julia thrust a note into her hand, explaining she was there only in case of an emergency. More an offer of support from the city's ruler as a way to strengthen the bond between the Hunters and Dwellers.

While Bianca was satisfied with Nicoletta's aftercare skills, as well as the woman's security prowess, she remained a trifle leery of her proficiency in a medical crisis. Presuming, given the Florentine's demise, Nicoletta's lack of suitable training was a contributing factor.

Bianca read the note and huffed, "If I have no other choice than to have you under foot, Julia, you might as well make yourself useful," refusing to acknowledge how much she appreciated the city's chief midwife being on standby.

Julia flashed the briefest of smiles. "I would not have it any other way, Miss Bianca."

The house was abuzz with a flurry of activity for the remainder of the day and well into the night. Bianca sat with her sister, trying to ease her anxiety.

Sophia was wont to weep over what she had said about Bianca and Gabriel's relationship.

"I never meant for you to think I would try to steal him away," Sophia sobbed. "Yes, I love Gabriel, but like the brother we never—"

"Hush, Sophia. I already know that. Besides, you are not

woman enough to come between us." Bianca chuckled and patted Sophia's hand.

"Bitch," was Sophia's response as they hugged.

"Yeah, yeah, and now we've settled that nonsense, let's get that baby delivered, hopefully that'll stop you being so emotionally charged."

Sophia was still in labour when Angelo appeared in the master chamber. Without waiting to be invited, he pulled a chair to the side of the bed, clutched his mate's hand, and began feeding her ice chips.

To Bianca's well-concealed amazement, Angelo seemed to mature in front of her eyes, instinctively knowing how to care for his mate. Absent were the usual absurdities which dripped from his lips like cheap wine from a drunkard.

Seriousness was the name of the game for the man.

An attitude Bianca welcomed, given Sophia's slow progress. Eighteen hours into Sophia's labour, Bianca decided it was time to apply the tinctures under her sister's tongue to hasten the delivery, in the manner Noemi had taught her.

The medicine worked its magic.

Within four hours, the babe had begun to crown.

Compared with Aurora's traumatic arrival into the world, the birth of Sophia's child was plain sailing. Despite Sophia cursing Angelo with everything from being flayed with a blunt knife, to being hung by his balls from the roof, she did not loosen her grip on his hand, and his soft words of encouragement did not stop.

Just when Sophia thought she had no more strength, it was over.

"You have a son," Bianca announced as she handed the baby to Nicoletta who cleaned the infant and swaddled him in a blanket.

Angelo, still holding Sophia's hand, twisted on the chair to stare at Bianca, his face one huge beam of unmitigated joy. "Really?" he croaked, overwhelmed.

Bianca nodded. "Really." Then, bending close so Sophia could not hear, cautioned, "Do not blow this."

Without waiting for his response, Bianca turned her attention to Sophia, while Nicoletta and Julia examined the baby — whose wailing proclaimed he had a pair of healthy lungs — checking whether he had the correct number of fingers and toes... among other things.

Then they reunited the child with his ecstatic parents.

Exhausted, Sophia brushed a kiss to the newborn's forehead.

For the sake of the city's birth records, Julia asked, "Have you decided on a name yet?"

Before Sophia could answer, Angelo interjected, "His name will be Giulio." He held his mate's gaze. "If you have no objection?"

Tears of happiness rolled down Sophia's cheeks.

"How could I say no?" She wept. "I'll wager my father would be honoured that his grandchild bears his name."

Bianca whispered into her brother-in-law's ear, "If ever there was a perfect time to show your authority in this relationship, this was it."

"Does that mean you will stop harassing me?" Angelo chuckled.

"Not in your wildest dreams." Bianca's snappy comeback was belied by her gentle squeeze of his shoulder.

8

Time and circumstance prevented the Padrona of the Hunters from resting as she ought to have done. No sooner had she bonded with her son, than Callixtus was on the doorstep requesting an audience.

Sophia had to admire his fortitude. Turning up without invitation, regardless of his lofty position, meant risking Bianca's wrath at disturbing a brand-new mother, scant hours after giving birth. It took a brave man to run *that* gauntlet.

Despite being propped up on a veritable cloud of pillows, Sophia managed to maintain her dignity and aura of being in control, while she accepted Callixtus' congratulations.

"Thank you, I admit to being exhausted and euphoric," she could not resist a sly dig, which sailed right over the chancellor's head, "but I am sure your presence here this morning is not solely to offer your good wishes."

Callixtus dipped his head in wry acknowledgement. "You are correct, my dear Padrona. While I prefer not to trouble you, at this... sensitive... time, delaying our discussion could have catastrophic repercussions. Not to mention the events which brought you here in the first place."

Bianca came in, carrying a tray ladened with oatmeal, whole-wheat bread, and a couple of hard-boiled eggs. Nutrient-rich foods which, Noemi had drummed into her daughters, were essential for mother and infant alike.

As for their *guest,* Bianca added a bowl of nuts… a very small one at that.

"I thought you might appreciate some refreshments." She fixed Callixtus with a hard stare. "Please do not tire Sophia. I know this is important, but she's just had a baby. You men have zero clue as to the battering our bodies take during childbirth…"

"*Bianca,*" Sophia exclaimed, her cheeks burning.

"Don't, Bianca, me." Her sister wagged a finger. "I'm just watching out for you."

"I will take every care," Callixtus intervened before a sibling squabble broke out. "I am not a complete slave driver." He winked and the tension eased.

Shuffling to get more comfortable, Sophia breathed in the robust aroma of coffee and reached out to accept the large mug from Bianca. "Bliss," she said, sipping the heady brew. "Thank you, Bianca, you're a poppet."

Bianca's eyebrows shot under her hairline at this saccharine sweet endearment. "I know," she said primly, hoping Sophia was just winding her up, not succumbing to delirium caused by a hidden infection, "and don't you forget it." She left the two alone but didn't quite close the door.

"Sorry about Bianca, she's a bit overprotective at the moment."

"Nothing to apologise for. She has earned the right to be bossy."

His amusement faded. "Do not hesitate to let me know if you need a break. We have much to discuss."

Over the next several hours… randomly interspersed with feeding Giulio, and sustenance for themselves... and, perhaps — although Callixtus was *far* too much the gentleman to mention it — Sophia's sporadic thirty or forty winks… the pair exchanged information about the latest threat to an already precarious stability.

Every time Callixtus mentioned the name of the monsignor, currently riding roughshod over everyone else's territory, something niggled in the far recesses of Sophia's mind but, for the life of her, she could not pin it down.

Assuming it was irrelevant, but making a mental note to ask Bianca later, she let it go for now.

Satisfied with the progress of the meeting, Callixtus thought it an appropriate time to introduce what he acknowledged might be a somewhat controversial subject with Hunters' Padrona.

"…and as for the movement of my spies through your lands—"

The spoon Sophia was using, slipped from her fingers to land on the floor with a clatter.

"Ex*cuse me*?" her voice rose dangerously on the question, certain her ears deceived her.

"After Luca's committal into the city's vaults last night, Dario and I talked to his widow. She explained how it is possible to infiltrate the Palazzo Vecchio. Dario said he had discussed this with you and your security, in order to ensure their safe passage through your territory."

Slowly, Sophia set her tray on the bedcovers, leaned as close as she could to Callixtus, and said menacingly, "Look into my eyes, Dweller."

The corner of Callixtus' right eye twitched nervously as a bead of sweat trickled down his forehead. Even during the tenuous early days of the negotiations between the Hunters and Rome, Callixtus had never heard this tone in Sophia's voice.

"Does it *appear* I was aware of this folly? You had best pray your people make it across *our* lands undetected, else you will have a collection of headless corpses piled before your city gates."

She settled back against her pillows. "Never assume ***anyone*** speaks for me, not even my sister. Now, excuse yourself. I am weary of this prattle."

Discretion being the better part of valour, Callixtus, unwilling to exacerbate this unexpected turn of events, or face Bianca's ire at upsetting her sister, tipped his hat and took his leave.

While Sophia recuperated, the Hunters' encampment packed up and moved south to Rome. The decision did not come without a cornucopia of objections and second-guesses.

Many accused Sophia of being complicit with the Dwellers whom, they believed, posed a threat to the Hunters' way of life.

Was it not enough that we extended our welcome to include the padrona performing a ridiculous pre-burial ritual for the dead Florentine? Noemi would never permit such a travesty.

Adding insult to injury, now we are expected to help defend the Romans' precious city at the cost of our lands?

When handed a *fait accompli,* particularly one they deemed misguided, mules were less stubborn than the Hunters, and their vociferous protests while they packed were relentless.

His wife and child in Rome under Bianca's care, Angelo

had offered to take charge of the move, and realised it was up to him to quell the mutinous mutterings.

Calling a halt to all work, he convened a meeting of his fellow Hunters at the central bonfire. Standing on the last unpacked trestle table, Angelo brought the spur of the moment pow wow to order.

"Since when do you get to play padrona?" one of their number demanded.

"Since he started shacking up with the actual padrona," his friend sallied with a sly wink.

This provoked more grousing.

Hell's teeth, thought Angelo morosely, *they are worse than whiny brats.* Conveniently forgetting, once upon a time, he and his brother complained about every little change Noemi instigated.

Swallowing his exasperation, he raised his palms.

The bellyaching subsided — marginally.

In as conciliatory tone as he could summon up, and to the shock of his listeners, Angelo agreed, "I know. Who'd have thought I'd be standing here, as our padrona's mate, asking you to put aside our differences for the sake of the greater good. Hell, until the confrontation with the Dwellers, the greater good was how many beers I could drink in one night, and still stand up.

"Never mind that Sophia is the best thing *ever* to happen to me, we, as a community, have come a long way since those days. The relationship between the Dwellers and ourselves has improved substantially, however…" as he heard the grumbles of dissatisfaction starting again, "…I am not suggesting everything in the garden is rosy, and we ought, very definitely, to maintain our vigilance.

"I don't suppose the Dwellers are particularly happy about us being in such close proximity to them either. An entente works both ways."

Not entirely sure whether he was persuading them, he decided to impart a few more pertinent details, thus far known only to a select handful.

"You must understand, this was not a decision the padrona took lightly. She is very protective of our autonomy. The move to Rome is because of a growing threat from the north. Do you think the Florentines fled without good reason? Their city flourished, and they believed it was safe from marauders.

"The fact is that Florence was invaded and captured by a horde from Bologna, with little resistance. Possibly, according to Nicoletta, because they… the inhabitants… were planning some kind of celebration and lowered their guard.

"Their leader is Monsignor Carlyle Worthington, self-proclaimed Pope of Bologna, and sounds like a crackpot of the highest order. He murdered two of our own in cold blood and without trial. While in itself enough to warrant our undivided attention, we cannot hope to defend ourselves if the numbers quoted by the Florentines are credible—"

"Why do we not charge north and deal with them the way we always have, instead of cowering like gutless saps?" The question was posited in a gruff manner.

"It comes down to simple maths. They outnumber us… probably four to one. They have war machines and a vast array of weaponry at their disposal. If we face them with the support of Rome, the odds of survival are increased significantly. Never mind we have the protection of the walls.

"Of course, the choice as to whether you stay or go, is yours. While I cannot countenance the notion of leaving any of you here to face this foe alone, I refuse to force anyone to accompany us against their will.

"If there are those among you who prefer to stay to

protect our lands, I shall not stand in your way. Your presence here will also help to stall any movements south."

A muttering broke out among the ranks. Although tantamount to falling on their swords, in the eyes of the Hunters, an illustrious death was preferable to a coward's.

Dubious as to whether he was getting through to those with qualms as to the sense of the plan, Angelo paused.

Before he could continue, an angry voice shouted from the back of the crowd. "You ain't fooling anyone with yer flowery speech, Angelo. You ain't got the balls to make us wipe our backsides, never mind up sticks and move to that cesspit of a city. Get off yer soapbox yer damn pup."

A nervous laugh rippled through the listeners.

The heckler, Santino, was only ever happy when he was grouching about something. Angelo pinched the bridge of his nose. He might have known Santino would balk… probably more because he was expected to pull his weight, get off his good-for-nothing ass and do some work, than because the camp was moving.

Alongside Santino, Angelo spotted one of his cronies, Carlo, nodding and nudging the heckler with his elbow. They were like a double act, only not the fun kind. Problem was they could easily sway those who might be vacillating.

On cue, Carlo taunted, "Aye, ya windbag. If not for your mate, you'd still be digging latrines for the camp."

Undeterred, Angelo swallowed his irritation and appealed to their bond; the unspoken solidarity, forged by circumstance, and cemented by friendship.

"You're not wrong. I can't deny my past, nor am I about to justify my life to anyone. Let's face it, we were all young and stupid once, but that does not discount the fact that we are Hunters. We will always be Hunters. To align with the Dwellers is not a sign of surrender, or a declaration that we are submitting to their constitution. It is a temporary coalition to ensure we are not conquered by a mutual aggressor."

"Will we have to live inside the walls?" someone asked.

"Not necessarily, but you do understand that solid stone is a far tougher shield than a metal caravan?" Angelo grinned, trying to lighten the mood.

"Ha ha, smarty pants. Careful, you're getting so sharp you might cut yourself one of these days," another retorted, but the outrage which had been swirling around the camp was dissipating as the Hunters pondered their options.

The group threw out more questions, which Angelo answered as honestly as he could. He did not pretend it would be easy, or a smooth transition, aware the Hunters were an independent bunch, but his assertion that this was a request from Sophia, not an order, along with his pledge that each individual's choice would be respected whatever it was, seemed to convince his listeners as little else could.

Fancy promises were wasted on the Hunters, and threats merely inflamed any given situation. Somehow… and when he looked back on it, even Angelo was not sure how… he had hit the right note. A subtle blend of camaraderie and the inference that a damn good scrap was on the cards.

Clearly Sophia's influence had rubbed off on him.

9

Struggling with the confines of city life, Sophia decided to take Guilio and join Angelo in their caravan outside Rome's walls.

Although Bianca still mother-henned her — making sure Sophia did not overexert herself — being in a familiar environment, recuperating in her own bed, and tending to the matters of her people, accelerated the healing process.

Nicoletta and her scouts, informed Sophia of any incursions into their territory, but the latter was increasingly concerned about the ramifications of the intelligence Callixtus continued to share.

While astounded his spies had circumvented her people, sparing their lives… no doubt because of Dario, which, in itself, necessitated a quiet word… the information they gleaned was unsettling.

Reports, relayed through the Roman ruler, spoke of strange buildings arising from the ashes of central Florence, belching thick black smoke into the sky, transforming the shimmering azure into a hazy grey cloud.

The crops and vineyards for which the city was once

famed resembled an arid wilderness. All remaining citizens had been forced into slave labour, destroying the very fields they had tended so assiduously, all for the sake of whatever Worthington was building.

Destruction of this magnitude was incomprehensible to Sophia and Callixtus, yet numerous reports implied the madman currently in control of the historic city seemed to have a purpose for everything he did, despite acting like a petulant child.

While devising a strategy to crush the Bolognese dominated their meetings, it was not all business. Sophia was still recuperating, so the pair made an effort to intersperse the serious with lighter conversational vignettes.

On one such occasion, Callixtus, with Bianca's wholehearted approval, introduced Sophia to a rather exceptional camellia tea from a town near Florence.

To her own surprise, Sophia — a self-confessed coffeeholic — was enjoying the delicate brew, which, Callixtus explained, he had spirited out of Lucca's botanical gardens before Worthington's men levelled the town, destroying the last vestiges of the plant, developed by the Lucchesi horticulturists before the plague.

"Why did you feel it essential to take such drastic measures for tea?" Sophia asked curiously.

"This variety has so many health benefits, I thought 'procuring it', worth the risk." The chancellor air-comma'd *procuring it,* his expression wry.

"Unfortunately, with the death of Lucca's botanists, ironically, at the hands of Mother Nature, the very deity they swore to protect, who paid no heed in her vengeful rage…"

Sophia chuckled at this.

"…no one was left to cultivate new plants."

"Ok, colour me interested. What benefits?" she pressed, taking another sip.

"The blend is purported to improve blood pressure, lower cholesterol, restore antioxidant enzymes and even reduce enlargement of the heart."

"Wow, impressive," Sophia's tone was lightly teasing.

Callixtus grinned. "Most importantly, and something I know Bianca approves of, is that it induces a calming effect, a useful beverage in stressful situations."

"It is not bad," Sophia conceded, not quite converted, "and, yes, Bianca would doubtless agree it's good for one's health," she paused and shot him a sideways glance, "I still prefer coffee."

Amused, Callixtus revealed, "As do I, but I daresay Bianca will have my head if I pump you full of espressos."

Savouring another mouthful of the tea, Sophia said with reluctance, "Well, my friend, if we are done debating the virtues of tea over coffee, and vice versa…" she dropped a sly wink, "…perhaps we ought to return to the matter at hand."

"That would probably be a wise choice." Taking the dig in good part, Callixtus swallowed the dregs of his drink, startled when Sophia snatched the delicate, bone china cup from his hand and studied the leaves at the bottom.

"What in the world are you doing?" Callixtus stared at her in bemusement.

"Something I read in an ancient book from my mother's library,"

"What?" Callixtus queried unable, quite, to disguise his incredulity. "Instructions for diagnosing ailments by studying tea leaves? I thought that was an old wive—"

Sophia cut him short. "Not hardly, Dweller. Not even we Hunters are that talented. No, the book spoke of teaching the reader how to divine the future of whomever consumed the brew."

"And what does destiny hold for me?"

"A battle looms but, and more importantly, you'll never enjoy another cup of tea with me." She shot him an arch look.

"Hmmm... perturbing, yet insightful. Does it say why, besides the obvious?" Callixtus, enjoying the banter, parried.

Infusing a hint of hauteur into her tone, Sophia replied, "I am afraid that information remains with the sibyl sitting before you, although, its lack of zing... technical term," she clarified loftily at Callixtus' quirked eyebrow, "may be a contributing factor. A better sacrifice, say actual coffee, has the power to change that aspect of your future."

"I'll make sure to bring coffee next time."

"See that you do."

Mirth subsiding, they reverted to perusing the yellowed map of Florence and its surrounds.

Sophia tapped her index finger on the parchment. "Your people have done an admirable job surveying the perimeter, Chancellor, but I think it is our turn to infiltrate the city to determine what Worthington is building—"

"Excuse me?" Callixtus interjected, irked that the Hunters' padrona praised his intelligence network in one breath, then insulted it in the next.

"Have they not demonstrated their worth, never mind they are already in place. Castello di Guadagni is barely five kilometres from the city. Far enough away to avoid notice by Worthington's patrols, but close enough should their presence be required urgently."

"Do they resemble Hunters?" Sophia replied acerbically. "I believe not. Have you forgotten how we breached your city's defences not *once* but *twice*? If so, I am happy to remind you in detail."

The night of the fire, as well as Sophia's brazen rescue of Bianca and Gabriel from the gallows, was still discussed within the walls of Rome in hushed undertones, as though perpetrated by creatures from the bowels of Hell who might, at any time, strike again with the same ruthlessness.

Even though the Hunters had brokered a truce with the city, Callixtus' citizenry were lodging quietly voiced concerns about their presence. Keeping the fragile peace between Dweller and Hunter was like a game of chess, one he realised was as much of a challenge to the padrona as it was to himself.

Callixtus resorted to his experience as a politician, reasoning a dignified submission was more sensible than trying to win a losing argument.

"Fine," he relented, "but my men will remain stationed at the castello in case your people need to be rescued."

Sophia assured him, "By all means, Chancellor. I would not expect anything less."

It was her accompanying smile which gave rise to the notion that his people would be the ones led like sheep to the slaughter… not the Hunters.

Outside Florence

Footsore after their week-long journey, Nicoletta and Dante opted to spend the night at the Castello di Guadagni… a ramshackle ruin recently 'purloined' by a unit of Callixtus' soldiers, led by Dario.

This gave them time to plan their next move, not to mention bask in the luxury of a decent place to sleep as opposed to huddling against a wall, or an unsuspecting farm animal.

Feeling refreshed, Nicoletta and Dante made a point of

arriving at the city limit shortly after noon when vigilance is at its post-prandial laziest.

They came upon two guards, lounging on the hood of an abandoned vehicle, dressed in riot gear similar to that worn by the Roman City Guard when the Hunters attacked them... except their helmets. The latter they had, thoughtfully, removed in order to smoke something neither Hunter could identify, nor cared to find out.

"Halt," one of the guards commanded. "What are you doing outside the fields? I know they have not been cleared, so take your asses back there or suffer the consequ—"

Dante raised his hand, palm out, arrogance radiating off him. "Do we look like Dwellers, you twat? The only thing I will *ever* harvest is the heads of rogues like you. Now present us to your superior, so we may apply for employment."

The other guard deemed it unwise to appear before his captain with these two, even if they were kindred Hunters, especially considering the likelihood they were armed.

"You shall not pass until you relinquish your weapons and submit to a search."

"You lay one finger on either of us... *friend,*" Dante warned, "and if I do not strike you down, my woman will."

"Enough of your nonsense." The guard unsheathed his sword.

Dante clicked his tongue at the stupidity of the challenge, brandishing his blade before Nicoletta could stop him.

Unfazed by his invariably impetuous reaction, she drew her own weapon and joined him.

The clash was vicious. This was the first time the Hunters had faced an opponent equal in strength and ability.

Nicoletta sustained a slash to her upper arm, while Dante received a deep gash to his forehead, injuries which acted as a spur, not a brace.

Seeing the blood dripping from his mate's arm, a red haze

descended over Dante's vision, and he surrendered to his bloodlust. He slashed left and right, severing the heads of both men in one fell swoop. Berserkers would have fled in the face of so merciless an onslaught.

It took Nicoletta grasping his shoulder to halt his mania.

Blinded by fury, he swung around ready to attack whoever dared thwart him. A firm whack from the flat side of his wife's blade atop his head jerked him back to reality.

"I swear, Dante," Nicoletta sighed, "I'm going to have Sophia open your skull one day to see if your brain is wired correctly… or even there at all."

He grinned sheepishly as he removed his tunic to wipe the blood from his face, then bandage his head wound.

Studying the guards, Nicoletta had an idea. She looked at Dante. "Strip!"

Dante did not need telling twice. "Did my finess with a sword excite you that much, wife?" He shucked off the rest of his clothes before she could come to her senses.

Not fast enough.

"Hold your horses." Nicoletta rolled her eyes. "Firstly, we do not have time for that. Secondly, I need you to wash your handiwork out of their uniforms. We'll be needing them."

Dante's shoulders slumped. This was the second time they had been on manoeuvres and had not been able to celebrate their accomplishments. He turned puppy dog eyes on his mate.

Unable to resist his boyish charm, she capitulated with a huffed, "Fine, but just a quickie."

"I'll take it!"

The 'quickie' stretched out well into the afternoon, both Hunters ended up stained in the blood of their vanquished, reminiscent of their younger days when they bathed in the blood of the dead.

Parenthood had changed them.

Satiated, Nicoletta stretched like a cat, and shimmied sinuously along Dante's muscular body before thumping his chest and yawning, "Damn you're good. Not sure I can stand. So much for all that fitness training. Ooof," she protested as her joints popped and settled.

"My pleasure, my lady." Dante twinkled wickedly, dropping a kiss on her forehead. "Care for another round? No one says we need to get to Florence to—"

"Do not finish that sentence." She wagged a finger at her husband and pushed herself to her feet. "Bad enough we have to wash and dry those wretched uniforms, but now we have to bathe as well."

Cleaning the uniforms turned out to be easier than either Hunter expected. The river water seemed to wick the blood from the material with minimal effort.

Nicolette was moved to remark, "Clearly a lot of thought has gone into how much soldiers bleed, prompting the creation of this special fabric. If we happen across a spare bolt or two, I do believe I shall commandeer some to clothe you and the kids. Very user friendly."

"And it is black." Dante grinned, ignoring her jibe. "My favourite colour."

"What was that phrase they used in the ancient time? Oh yeah, aren't you the fashionista!"

"Well, a man has to look good." He puffed out his chest.

"Smug much? Watch your head, I think it's beginning to swell." Nicoletta did not bother to mask her amusement, as she hung the uniforms by the makeshift fire, impressed by how quickly they dried.

A boon, given they intended to slip into the city under the cover of darkness, and dusk was already sending long shadows across the ground.

10

The pair arrived at the city gates, helmets and face guards in place to shield their appearance from anyone they passed.

Much like their own camp, illumination came in the form of the same glaring, portable tower lights. Unlike the Hunters' compound, electricity to these was supplied by a noisy generator, rather than powered by solar collectors.

In a low voice Nicoletta observed, "We are supposed to be terrorised by their advanced technology? My only fear is the distinct possibility of being torn apart when those pieces of crap explode. They cannot even power a light correctly."

"Shut it, my love," Dante entreated, knowing it was a waste of breath, "and let me do the talking."

"No doubt straight into a dungeon, but don't let that stop you."

Approaching the Watch, Dante made some bizarre salute, confusing all present.

"Whose command are you under, soldier, and why are you returning at this hour? I do not believe any of the troops are scheduled to return until midday next," the guard, sporting enough brass on his chest to finance a small country asked, while his subordinate tried, and failed, to mask a sneer.

Ignoring the question, Dante reached into his knapsack to remove the heads of the guards he had decimated, ensuring their identity could never be ascertained. It was Nicoletta's spur of the moment idea to bring them in case they were challenged.

Tossing them at the feet of the Watch, Dante reported matter-of-factly, "We came across two Dwellers who had escaped the fields, apparently trying to make their way south. Something I am sure the monsignor…"

Dante and Nicoletta exhaled silent sighs of relief that Dante recalled the fancy title Worthington had bestowed upon himself.

"…will be displeased to know your detachment cannot do something as simple as monitor a bunch of *farmers*."

The man was too astounded at the brutality of the injuries inflicted on the skulls to care what the idiot in front of him had said. "For the love of our saviour, what is this mess? Was it your first kill, soldier? There is not enough left to fashion a half-assed trophy."

"I am very capable with puzzles and model assembly," Dante's facetious reply was mitigated… and, thankfully, lost on his questioner… by his dead pan expression.

Nicoletta pressed her lips together to stifle a bark of mirth, willing her mate not to drop a clanger, relieved when the sentry, blessed with little imagination, failed to register he was being mocked.

"Get these pieces of shit out of here." the bemedalled guard snapped.

Dante snatched the heads, stuffed them into the pack, and walked through the gate into the city.

When Nicoletta attempted to follow, the guard contested, "You… why is your uniform so ill-fitting?"

She shouldered past the man, grunting coarsely, "You try surviving on patrol with that lug and see how much weight *you* lose."

The pungent odour of decay, machinery grease, and exhaust fumes struck the pair, the moment they dared remove their helmets. Nicoletta replaced hers to stave off rising nausea.

Memories flooded her of the time, decades ago, when her father brought her to Florence on a bright sunny day to prowl the city unnoticed. Despite art appreciation being a trait missing from her people, the sounds and aromas had fascinated the girl.

To a child's eye, the sky which floated high above Florence appeared to be a brighter blue; the occasional vaporous cloud, whiter and fluffier than those which drifted over their camp. As day morphed into night, the countless stars, suspended in the obsidian darkness, twinkled like diamonds.

An emotion Nicoletta struggled to discern, teased at the periphery of her consciousness. Generally practical, she ignored it, but it lingered.

The residents of the city once numbered nigh on forty thousand, even after the plague. If she had to guess, Nicoletta reckoned the population was reduced to a third — tops. Of those, the majority were little more than skeletal shells of their former selves, wandering aimlessly in shabby, tattered clothing.

Hands wrapped in blood-soaked rags spoke of labour

forced upon them at the whim of those who would not recognise an honest day's work if it slapped them upside the head. Faces, gaunt and pale, were stained in the same soot which spewed from the hastily erected chimneys littering the city.

Nicoletta studied the features of those they passed; a sea of sunken gazes averted. Did they fear retribution for daring to meet the eye of a soldier?

The couple circled a series of camps, set up haphazardly wherever the displaced citizens could find shelter.

Seeing a woman change direction to skirt the 'soldiers', Nicoletta grasped her arm. Almost forgetting her disguise, Nicoletta's question sounded oddly rough, "Why are you people in the streets? Has there been some disaster?"

The woman tried to wrench her arm from Nicoletta's grip but did not possess the strength.

Unable to stem weak tears, she protested, "Is it not enough that Monsignor Worthington has confiscated our homes to accommodate your troops, only for you to mock me with your feigned concern? You should be ashamed of yourself."

She stifled a sob. "Please, allow me to be on my way while there are still blankets left to be had. Even a moment's delay might cost me the chance to secure a tent."

Nicoletta released her hold but, watching the woman disappear into the crowd of equally hopeless people, realised the nagging sentiment was no longer unidentifiable.

It was an all-pervasive bereavement; an echo of unutterable tragedy, wrought by the death of this beautiful city. "That bastard Worthington has stolen the very heartbeat of this place," she murmured sadly for to speak any louder seemed… irreverent.

The compassion in his wife's declaration caught Dante off-guard. The closest he had come to visiting Florence was an occasional foray into the outlying fields. Her sympathy for these Dwellers was new to him.

That in their younger days, they had taken the lives of people such as these, indiscriminately, left him without a witty rebuttal. Opting for discretion… doubtless a temporary aberration… he looped his arm through hers and led her to the closest building complete with smokestack.

Their uniforms proved to be the perfect disguise, allowing the pair to blend in with the guard during the change of Watch, which was conducted in a hermetically sealed room, spared from the pollution emanating from the machinery on the manufacturing floor below.

Huge, angled windows had been installed allowing a team of wardens to monitor the area, and minimising direct contact at the production level.

As the crew of the third shift prepared to draw lots, relegating the loser to the first shift, Dante and Nicoletta stepped forwards to volunteer.

"We'll take the first round," Dante offered, making sure to keep his voice gruff and his tone grudging.

The shift leader studied them, unaware or, and more likely, uncaring that he had acquired two more peons. If they were willing to expose themselves to lung contamination in his place, so be it.

"Make sure you take care of yourself, boy," the commander warned. "Second shift had to put down a handful of them peasants. Seems they had a deluded idea they could take us on."

"Yes, sir," Dante replied, clicked his heels, and turned to

leave the control room, only to be halted when the commander shouted, "Soldier. About face."

Unsure why he was being reprimanded, Dante spun on his heel to see the man standing with his fist over his heart. Dante made sure to mimic the gesture.

"I know it is a worthless formality, soldier, but it is one the monsignor requires, and one you'd best not forget. I should hate to include you in the next batch of the dead." The commander scowled.

"I apologise, sir. Thank you for correcting me."

Nicoletta and he flashed the appropriate salute before descending the wooden stairs to the fire and kilns.

Left to their own devices, Nicoletta and Dante patrolled the factory, taking care not to draw attention to themselves.

The pair explored the mill-room first where they discovered teams of men and women harnessed to wooden beams attached to large quern stones. As far as the Hunters could deduce, the Dwellers were not granted any breaks during their shifts.

If water was needed, someone — hidden from view — released it from an overhead vat, soaking everyone underneath.

From the rough mill-wheel, the pulverised grapes and vines, once the pride of this city, were conveyed along a belt to a series of treadmills. The individuals chained to these crude machines were required to climb a set of stairs continually, ensuring the fruit and greenery was reduced to a mash which was shovelled into huge vats, ready for conversion to biodiesel.

If any of the slaves tethered to either system stumbled or

lost consciousness from overexertion, they were cut from the harnesses and replaced.

Dante saw one after another hauled through a door at the far side of the production floor but, in the relatively short time he and Nicoletta were there, none returned.

The scene reminded Nicoletta of childhood stories about English workhouses, and, irrespective of the fact these hapless victims were dwellers and her historical enemy, she was beset by an uncharacteristic urge to protect them.

At the end of the shift, the pair were relieved and instructed to return to the control room; an order they elected to ignore. Instead, they slipped out of the factory, intent on exploring the other processing plants.

Outside, the duo stripped off the invaders' uniforms, and changed back into their own dirty clothes, which they had stuffed into their packs.

Prior to recent events, their usual attire would mark them as non-Dwellers, but no longer. The bedraggled clothing of the city's inhabitants meant the newcomers blended in with ease, and no one questioned their presence at the displaced residents' camp.

The Hunters gleaned a wealth of information, such as the rotation of the guards, what was expected of the civilians, and the location of the armouries.

As morning approached, Nicoletta and Dante changed into their uniforms to merge with those soldiers sent to rouse the Florentines for a new day of *voluntary service* for the monsignor.

A routine the couple repeated during the next three days, becoming well-versed in the city's layout. While Fortune had favoured them until now, almost the moment husband and wife agreed it was time to withdraw, she left them stranded.

Worthington's men paid a visit to the encampments in the darkest hour, just before dawn when reactions of those disturbed would be at their most sluggish. The guards ransacked the makeshift shelters, searching for something or someone in particular.

The captain of the guard barked, "Find them or it will be your heads on the city gates. If any of these rabble dare hide them, see to it they are made an example of."

The entire exercise was a demonstration of the monsignor's control over Florence. He already knew which of the camps the pair had frequented, located on city lands outside a defunct Catholic church.

Their location betrayed for a few scraps of bread.

The monsignor chuckled to his personal bodyguard. "The world used to think gold was the most valuable commodity and murdered each other for it. Little did they know, all possessed it many times over.

"Food, my friend, that was all they ever needed. Fools... all of them."

His words were lost on the man whose only purpose was to sacrifice his own life for Worthington.

Inwardly, the megalomaniac bemoaned the days when he could carry on a conversation with someone who possessed even a modicum of his own intelligence. "That was expecting a miracle," he conceded.

Dismissing the thought, Worthington, a crossbow slung over his shoulder, ascended the rickety stairs of a convenient bell tower, determined to reach the top before his men made their presence known.

From the safety of his battlement, he removed a pair of antique binoculars from a leather case bearing the name *General George Patten* — a soldier with whom Worthington identified and whose auctioned possession had cost him a pretty penny decades ago… an outlay he never regretted — and watched his men burst into the courtyard below.

As the inhabitants of the camp scurried to grab whatever belongings they could, Worthington trained his binoculars on two figures sprinting to the road which led to Rome.

"There you are." He smiled. "How dare you leave my city without a suitable souvenir."

Locking a bolt into the crossbow, he levelled it at the smaller of the two. Inhaling and holding his breath, he released the metal arrow.

His aim was true. The four-pronged dart buried itself into the leg of the fleeing trespasser, spinning him — the monsignor presumed both were male; that one might be a woman never entered his misogynistic head — around and felling him.

Worthington's intent was not to kill, but his message was clear; no one was allowed in any of his cities without a formal invitation.

Despite his conviction that the pair were comrades, Worthington expected to see the uninjured male abandon his companion, astonished when he did not.

Instead, the former lifted the latter, and hefted him over his shoulder, before resuming his mad dash for freedom.

No way does he have the strength to escape carrying that dead weight, Worthington mused.

Watching his men close in on the pair, Worthington sent out a signal, calling off the pursuit.

He snapped the lid shut on his binocular case. "Let us see whether we garner some guests with that send off."

11

Nicoletta draped over his shoulder, Dante raced towards sanctuary but, with his wife writhing and screaming, the five-kilometre dash to their allies felt like a never-ending marathon — the edge of the universe seemed closer.

It was obvious to Dante that, given Nicoletta was not dead, whoever had shot his woman in the shin was either an embarrassingly poor marksman or, possessed the expertise to cripple her in a deliberate attempt to impede them.

The notion plagued him, but he had no time to dwell on the whys and wherefores right now. Right now, his priority was getting Nicoletta to safety.

The Hunter's destination... Castello di Guadagni.

The castello had stood its ground for nigh on a millennium, surviving umpteen man-made catastrophes, as well as any number of visits from the Third Horseman of the Apocalypse... Pestilence.

Regrettably, and despite its long history, in more recent times the chateau's long and charmed existence expired.

The most devastating plague ever conceived by humanity,

claimed not only the lives of those who called this place home — including generations of the noble family, estate workers, and, curiously, the livestock — it had ravaged the castle itself.

With no one left to maintain it, the Castello di Guadagni had fallen into disrepair, even the barbarians of old could not have laid against it a more destructive siege.

The façade of the once gleaming white structure was now strewn in ribbons of rubble along the withered stubble of formerly manicured hedges radiating out from the long destroyed grand entrance.

The desecration of the castello suited its current occupants, the Roman city guard, who had no problem requisitioning the crumbling ramparts to use as barricades.

It was over one of these great chunks of stone, Dante stumbled. Exhausted beyond reason, he collapsed in a heap, still clutching his bleeding wife.

Her agonised wails galvanised the entirety of the guard. Seconds later, Dante and Nicoletta were surrounded by an anxious throng who whisked them through the gates and into the villa before either could attempt to stand.

Dante heard a woman's voice barking out commands.

"Get her to the surgical table, and someone administer an IV, A-SAP."

While the orders sounded as though they were issued by Bianca, the accent was different. Turning his head before darkness claimed him, Dante glimpsed the woman he had met at Bianca and Gabriel's villa. It was Julia, the Roman chancellor's personal physician.

With a relieved smile, Dante succumbed to oblivion.

Ignoring the hulking male, Julia concentrated on Nicoletta. Deftly, the newly assigned field surgeon clipped off the arrow's mechanical head, which had splayed open after passing through the Hunter's shin.

She made sure not to touch the metal tips in case they had been dipped in toxins. Aware of the devious nature of their enemy, chicanery could not be disregarded.

Dropping the barb into a bowl, Julia asked one of the guards, who she was training, to test the metal for any known poisons… or the presence of any other lethal substance.

Julia extracted the shaft as gently as possible, then cleaned and sutured the wound, marvelling at its location which, while excruciatingly painful and resulting in a decent loss of blood, had not damaged the bones and was not life threatening.

Finished, and awaiting the toxicology report, Julia examined the Hunter for any further injuries. The young surgeon knew that if she sent the woman home without following the fundamental tenets, Bianca had drummed into her students so vigorously, she would suffer her teacher's wrath.

Julia ran light fingers along Nicoletta's extremities, noting what felt like some kind of padding just below her patient's shoulder. Opening the woman's tunic, she discovered her assumption was correct.

She frowned at the ragged bandage, which, although not soaked in blood — doubtless owing to the Hunter's training in emergency wound treatment — clearly, had not been changed since the injury occurred.

"For the sake of the Holies, woman, did you skip Bianca's lessons on aftercare?" Julia chided to the unconscious Nicoletta. "It is fortunate you ended up on my table, for this laceration is likely to become septic."

Conscientiously, Julia removed the strapping, striving to avoid tearing any scabbing.

Despite her best efforts, blood seeped from what the medic diagnosed to be a sword slash. Rinsing the gash with saline from her supply, she sewed it closed, then slathered a sizeable dollop of a medicated salve, lauded and thus taught to all and sundry by Bianca, over the wound before applying a piece of gauze and a fresh dressing.

Satisfied she had staved off the female's untimely demise, Julia turned to the male. Unlike the woman, his bandages were relatively clean and secured in place with care and expertise.

Unwrapping the binding, she observed a neatly stitched lesion at the centre of a nasty contusion. To accomplish such a delicate procedure on oneself was impossible, meaning the female had patched up both of them. Quite a feat given they had limited resources.

Julia tutted to herself, "Evidently, your mate was more concerned with your well-being than her own."

"She did not want to be left alone with the twins," Dante interjected laconically, opening his eyes, slowly. Instinctively, he swung his legs over the edge of the cot and attempted to stand, determined to check on Nicoletta, then find Dario.

As shaky feet touched the floor, a firm hand gripped his arm to prevent him from taking another step.

"No, you don't."

Reading his thoughts, Julia added, "Your mate is well but sleeping, and her physician refuses to allow you to wake her. Rest here, and I will summon the captain so you can speak with—"

On cue, Dario appeared at the door, his expression wry. "Is he alive?"

"Yes, dear brother, I am currently listed among the living, thanks, I guess, to this martinet…" tipping his head at Julia grudgingly "…who won't let me check on Nic. Please explain that my wife will thrash the living daylights out of everyone within reach if she does not see me as soon as she regains consciousness." Dante's complaint was not without merit… if a trifle exaggerated.

As someone who had borne the brunt of his sister-in-law's outbursts on more than one occasion, Dario chuckled. "I am sure my learned surgeon will ensure your surly consort does not wake enough to cut a swathe through my men until such time as you are fit to move."

Dante's mouth twisted in sardonic amusement. "On your head be it. Talk about jumping in where angels fear to tread, you enjoy flirting with danger?"

"Me? You are the one who married the she-beast… and was crazy enough to give her kids."

"No worse than joining the Dwellers and courting disaster at the hands of the Bolognese," Dante countered superciliously. "Speaking of the unwelcome occupant of Florence… care to explain how it is you and the Romans are within spitting distance of the city centre, yet have not been obliterated by his war machines?"

"Luck, maybe?" Dario mused. "Or maybe he heard who commands this expedition and is terrified to face me," he said, unconsciously straightening his shoulders.

Dante spluttered with mirth at Dario's tone which bordered on the pompous. "Careful, brother. You do not suit a swagger and, if you puff your chest out anymore, Julia here might be tempted to prick you with one of her needles and release some of that hot air."

About to refute his sibling's jibe, Dante heard himself and joined in the laughter. Briefly, they bantered back and forth, in a manner almost forgotten.

Then, as was their custom when matters needed to be hashed out, their discussion became serious.

"Hindsight being what it is," Dante reasoned, as he sipped some of the ancient cognac Dario deemed sensible to snaffle from a long-abandoned case he had stumbled across in a derelict storage room, "Gabriel's decision to destroy Rome's main armoury may not have been the wisest choice."

"True," his brother agreed, "it does leave us at a distinct disadvantage. From what we have been able to deduce, Worthington outguns us by a good two to one but, without access to any oil fields, his armoured weaponry won't be of much—"

"Think again," Dante interrupted. "Those noxious clouds being spewed out of his newly constructed smokestacks are from the biofuels he is terrorising the Florentines into producing. It appears Worthington is not going to fall victim to the same mistakes as his predecessors when they stretched their forces beyond the limits of their supply lines. Have to give the lunatic credit for being a student of history and a forward thinker."

"If you are done fanboying Worthington," Dario grumbled, "perhaps you can come up with a plausible scheme to drive him out of the city."

"Off the top of my head, I have nothing but a nagging question. Why not kill us? The shot to Nic's leg illustrates the skill of his marksmen… not to mention your platoon's continued existence here unchallenged. Do you suppose he is biding his time, perhaps hoping the padrona might be open to some kind of covenant?"

"Instead of an outright war? Maybe, but who's to say?"

"Do you think the sisters are willing to risk a repeat of our conflict with the Romans?"

"No." Dario settled back in his chair, swirling his cognac, letting it breathe. "No, while the two do not shy away from a good battle, neither want to squander lives for a losing cause."

"Then I propose we burn the city to the ground, and not bother telling either of them," an angry voice from the doorway caught their attention.

Balanced on a set of crutches stood Nicoletta, fire raging

in her eyes. "Whichever fucker shot me deserves to have his ass torched."

An equally angry Julia appeared behind the Hunter. "I told you not to get out of bed."

On her one good foot, Nicoletta spun around, coming face to face with the surgeon. "How would you like a crutch up the side of your head, Dweller?"

"Is that before or after I introduce it to your hind end?"

Nicoletta fell silent, racking her brain for a similarly stinging retort. While she had encountered more than a few Dwellers willing to spout some inanity at the risk of their heads, she had never met a civilian quite as cavalier with their lives as this woman seemed to be.

Unable to come up with a blistering comeback, Nicoletta sized Julia up for a solid smack, aiming to shatter the crutch over her opponent's head.

Dante rose from his chair to intercede. "Ladies, ladies, please. Spare us from unnecessary violence within our ranks and direct it at the Bolognese."

The others chuckled at his, admittedly weak, attempt at playing peacemaker… quickly diffusing the volatility between patient and physician.

Pushing past Dante, Nicoletta bagged his chair, and propped up her foot on a nearby stool.

"So, brother-in-law, if you and my husband ever decide to cobble together a battle plan… don't."

Finishing his drink, Dario retorted, "Well, sister-in-law, you were the one who just proposed we storm the barricades."

"Blame that on your surgeon's drugs," Nicoletta shot back, grimacing at Julia. "Putting that aside, maybe getting the padrona and Worthington to sit at the same table is not the worst idea… under a white flag."

"You mean surrender to the bastard?" Dante blurted out, astonished his wife would suggest such a thing.

"Don't be daft," she reassured, "but it would be good to glean what the maniac has in mind."

Shuffling in the chair, to make herself more comfortable, Nicoletta gave Dario an order in the guise of a suggestion, "How about sending one of your riders to Rome to fetch our leader."

"I have just the person, but what about Callixtus?"

Tapping her chin with her index finger, Nicoletta contemplated the chancellor's fate if he accompanied Sophia.

"That's your call, Dario. Your *friend* is not a Hunter, if you think it wise to jeopardise his health…" she left that dangling. "And who is 'just the person'?"

"Antonio." Dario sat back and waited for the fireworks.

Stunned, Nicoletta did not fail him. "*Antonio*? Since when?" she expostulated, as Dante's mouth opened and closed like a stranded trout.

"He and I came to an… arrangement… he's a brilliant scout."

"Firstly, I never expected to hear Antonio and brilliant scout in the same sentence. Secondly, how long has he worked for you and who came up with such a crackpot idea? Hell, Sophia will go ballistic." Nicoletta's tone bordered on the incredulous.

"Do you take me for an idiot? Sophia knows. I asked whether he could be seconded to my unit for a stint. My men are less than clear about the Hunters' boundaries, and I can't be everywhere. He's been an excellent deputy."

"Well, bugger me." Dante found his voice and blew out his cheeks. "I never thought I'd see the day when not one but two of our own, aided and abetted an erstwhile enemy."

"It's a good relationship, Dante. The stronger the links between the Hunters and the Romans the more effective we will be against a common enemy." Dario waved his hand in the general direction of Florence. "Case in point."

Nicoletta and Dante were silent, ruminating over this extraordinary revelation, conceding that Dario was not erroneous in his reasoning… *but Antonio? Who knew he had a brain?*

None of them noticed the pink stain creeping up Julia's face, and she was certainly not about to elaborate.

12

A Week Later

Three men walked abreast of the donkey hitched to the wagon carrying their families. Antonio led his horse who — had anyone known it — was very relieved not to be ridden at breakneck speed all the way back to the castello.

Bianca had declared Julia was not equipped to manage multiple casualties, and no amount of persuasion from Gabriel could deter her from accompanying Sophia. Not prepared to let his adored wife disappear off into the wilds of Italy, Gabriel packed his bags.

Angelo's attempts to convince Sophia to leave Giulio with one of the camp's wet nurses for safety's sake fell on deaf ears. The new mother had no intention of entertaining that notion.

Which led to Aurora using her childish wiles to inveigle *her* way into the party.

This triggered pleas — accompanied by a series of pouts, strategically interspersed with hopeful looks from tear-filled eyes — from Rocco and Zara to be included because they missed their parents, prompting an early departure to avoid a reprisal of their dramatic performance.

The presence of Aurora and Giulio warranted extra personnel in the form of guards who rode at the rear. To say all the men were armed to the teeth was an understatement. As well as their usual swords, each carried a semi-automatic rifle procured, under the eagle eye of Antonio, from what remained of the Roman armoury.

In the bed of the wagon — within easy reach of the passengers, should a band of witless wonders with hero complexes decide to ambush the party en route — a large tarpaulin concealed a cache of weapons, earmarked for the current occupants of the castello.

The consensus of the travellers was that a white flag probably meant little to someone as barbarous as Worthington, but pre-apocalyptic firepower would certainly grab his attention.

Bianca, glancing over her shoulder at the hidden cargo, grilled her sister, "Pray tell, how did you persuade Callixtus to cough up so many rifles, especially after you told him he could not come to the meeting with Worthington?"

Her gaze fixed on the road ahead, Sophia did not reply.

"You *did* tell him where we are going?"

There was a brief and somewhat loaded silence, then Sophia confided, "Not in so many words."

"How many words did you use, Sophia?" Bianca quirked a quizzical brow at her duplicitous sibling.

"None."

"What?" Bianca squawked. "Then how on earth did you secure these weapons?"

"Placating the chancellor is not the only talent Dario employs," Sophia replied with a devious smile; one Bianca had never seen before. "Seems they extend to wheedling pertinent information from our dear, dear Callixtus… such as the combination to their armoury's padlock, which he saw fit to pass on to Antonio."

"When did you become such a mastermind?" Bianca did not know whether to be exasperated or impressed.

"Have we not always taken what we needed?"

"Point taken, but not usually from those with whom we are allied."

"Bah," Sophia scoffed and, jerking a nod at Angelo's back, gave an impish grin. "Blame my mate there. He is surprisingly enterprising when circumstances demand. Must have rubbed off on me."

The sun was kissing the horizon when the weary travellers — jaded and dusty from what was beginning to feel like a never-ending journey — reached the gateway to the castello. The dying rays of the flaming orb, shooting into a sky morphing from blue to purple, turned the patches of rust clinging to the ancient metal scrollwork into delicate embellishments of burnished gold.

Gabriel jiggled the latch securing the twin, ten-foot, iron behemoths but it held fast, refusing entry to any who were not invited.

"Anyone home?" he called, shrugging at his wife who rolled her eyes. "Well, what else am I supposed to say?"

Sophia hopped down and rattled the gates.

"***Dario,***" her unladylike bellow echoed off the high walls and reverberated around the turrets. "Get your ass here this instant."

They heard the sound of scurrying feet, then a pale face

peered through the gate, and a shrill voice demanded, "Who goes there?"

"And you are?" Sophia's reply carried a dangerous edge. She was tired, cold, hungry, and now irritated. Her body ached from being jostled in that wretched cart, and now some pipsqueak expected her to identify herself.

If this was an example of the Roman city guard, they were right royally screwed. "Who do you imagine might call at this hour? A king?"

Angelo came alongside, looped his arm around her waist and murmured in her ear, "Be reasonable, my love, we cannot know what they have faced."

Had anyone else asked Sophia to 'be reasonable', it is probable her response would involve sharp implements yet, somehow, Angelo's tone soothed her temper.

"I am not feeling reasonable." Sophia knew Giulio would begin his ritual wailing if she didn't feed him soon; the infant was voracious.

Her mind went off on a tangent. Hopefully this meant he would grow into a tall strapping lad, like his father. She raked her gaze over Angelo's muscular frame and felt her vexation ease at the prospect of being in his arms. *Drat it all, what happened to, I don't need a man?* her cynical side scorned — to be flipped the bird by sentiment.

"I know, but that's not this young man's fault."

Sophia dragged her mind back and gave a disgruntled *harumph*, but, conceding Angelo was not wholly incorrect, pinned on a smile to explain with saccharine sweetness, "Please inform Commander Barzetti, that Sophia Ricci, Padrona of the Hunters and her entourage have arrived and would appreciate being granted access."

The youth's eyes widened. *Dammit, not the person I ought to be upsetting.* He hastened to unlock the gate, his fingers fumbling with the great bolt. It clanged back and he tugged hard, the aged metal shrieking in protest.

A tall figure appeared around the side of the cart. "Panic not, Vito, I can vouch for the new arrivals."

Recognising Antonio, Vito relaxed… marginally. If Commander Barzetti's deputy said they were ok, that was fine by him. "Evening, Antonio." He bowed his head respectfully.

"A little oil would not go amiss." Angelo nodded at the hinges. "That's loud enough to disturb the dead, never mind any enemy scouts who might be lurking in the vicinity."

"I'll see to it," the youth stammered, awe written all over his face. He had heard of Sophia and her confrontation with the previous rulers of Rome.

His gaze swept across the rest of the party, to land on another woman, so similar to Sophia they *had* to be related, surmising her to be Bianca, which meant the tall man at her elbow was Gabriel. This couple were the stuff of legends.

Unable to help himself, Vito actually bowed as the four walked through the gate. "Welcome to Castello di Guadagni," he greeted belatedly.

"Thank you." Bianca smiled as she passed. "Don't mind Sophia," she whispered with a wink. "She's the grumpy one."

"I heard that," Sophia retorted.

Bianca and the young man shared a grin, then he dashed ahead to lead the way to the grand entrance.

Pushing open the huge doors, the young man announced in far more stentorian tones than he had yet employed, "Sophia Ricci, Padrona of the Hunters. Bianca and Gabriel, renowned revol…" he thought better of it, "…reformists and peacemakers."

There was a kind of surge as people appeared from every direction, the first to reach the new arrivals, Dario, with Dante on his heels and Nicoletta not far behind.

"Finally. I was beginning to think you had got lost," Dante teased.

"Watch it." Sophia punched him in the shoulder, spotting her chief of security on crutches. "What the hell happened?"

"Long story." Nicoletta grimaced. "Come on, let's get you settled, then we'll fill you in."

Two hours later, freshened up, children fed and tucked into bed, bellies full, and drinks served, Sophia and co. listened with horror to Dante's description about what was unfolding inside Florence, and their growing concern that the city's demise might be the latest in a long line similarly afflicted by Worthington's devious machinations.

It was far worse than even Callixtus had anticipated.

"The man is a lunatic," Angelo said when Dante had finished.

"Understatement of the decade," Nicoletta grumbled, "but, if we can flatter his ego and lull him into a false sense of security, we might be in with a chance of stopping him."

"Are we free to enter the city, or do we risk capture?" Sophia asked.

"If we infer you," Dante waved his hand at the newcomers, "are an envoy from Rome, hoping to discuss a treaty with Worthington, you ought to reach him unmolested."

"Let me go," Nicoletta interjected. "That man and I are due a chat."

Julia opened her mouth to remind Nicoletta she was supposed to be in bed, not delivering verbal… or otherwise… broadsides, but Bianca got there first.

"Not on your Nelly." The physician wagged a stern finger. "Firstly, you are not fit, secondly, you and I both know this will not end well, and Sophia needs you alive."

There was a brief battle of wills, which Bianca was never going to lose.

Slumping into her chair, Nicoletta grumbled balefully

under her breath. In truth, she felt wretched; her leg throbbed, and her head ached — not that she was prepared to admit to either.

Sophia leant across to murmur, "You are not letting me down, Nic. You and Dante have already gone above and beyond. Without you, we would be going in blind and deaf. Fret not, I shall let you take his head should circumstance permit." Her grin was nothing short of devilish.

Nicoletta chuckled ruefully. "Fair enough."

The discussion continued until well after midnight, suggestions becoming more bizarre in direct correlation with the amount of excellent red wine being imbibed.

Eventually, Bianca put a stop to it, dispatching everyone to bed like a mother hen. "The way you lot are emptying bottles, the only thing you'll get out of this is a sore head. Off with you." Hands on hips, shaking her head in exasperation, she watched them traipse out to their respective quarters.

Gabriel came up behind her, wrapped his arms around her waist and pillowed his chin on her glossy hair. "They needed to let off some steam, better with wine than weapons."

"I know, but an all-nighter? None of us can bounce back from one of those like we used to." Bianca blew a tired sigh. "That said, I do think Dante's idea of an envoy could work." She tapped her chin thoughtfully.

"Worthington will preen at the notion that the chancellor of Rome is interested in some kind of accord. He'll think he has the upper hand, lulling him into that false sense of security, Nicoletta mentioned. In the meantime, maybe between us we can find the chink in his armour."

"Let's sleep on it." Gabriel yawned and belched. "Sorry."

"You are a shocker," Bianca scolded, even as her gaze softened. "Come on, doubtless Aurora will be up with her namesake, which is scant hours away.

Before long, save the ceaseless patrols, the castello fell quiet.

Sophia determined simple was best. The more complicated the plan, the more likely it was to go wrong, or unravel.

Bianca, Gabriel, and a contingent of Romans would follow Sophia's group at a discreet distance to set up a staging post mid-way between the castello and the city. Partly to act as an early warning system for those waiting at the ruins, and partly as an advanced surgical post.

Given Dante and Nicoletta were known to Worthington and his cronies, their involvement had to be minimal and, in Nicoletta's case, non-existent.

Chafing at being side-lined, Dante was slightly mollified when Sophia proposed he take charge of the weaponry.

"Now you know how I feel," Nicoletta groused, then met Sophia's eyes, dipping her head in acknowledgement of what she read there.

"These probably need testing," she tossed out airily, lifting the tarpaulin to run her hand over the various armaments in the back of the cart. "Ohhhh, nice."

Dante took the bait and, his humour restored, began to lift out and examine each piece.

Sophia grinned at her security chief, waved her goodbyes, and set off accompanied by those elected to parlay with the monsignor.

The small entourage, so as not to seem intimidating, consisted of Sophia, Angelo, Julia in her capacity as medic, Dario, and two guards — who, Dario informed her, were called Massimo and Aldo — attired in full uniform, medals gleaming.

To Sophia's badly concealed amusement, Angelo and Dario argued nearly the whole of the short journey about who was the better mediator.

Tuning them out, she scrutinised her surroundings, seeing what Nicoletta and Dante as well as Callixtus' scouts had described.

In the distance, the city was shrouded in a dirty grey haze. The fields, once fertile, were barren.

Sophia frowned.

From where was Worthington getting his fodder for the biofuel, now? If he had cleared the fields, he must be running out of raw materials.

As she puzzled over this, staring out over the scourged landscape, a frisson of dread snaked through her.

Was this his intention? To use the whole of Italy as one huge resource? Creating an unstoppable force of men and machines as he went. Capturing or killing any who tried to thwart him.

Sophia had heard her mother talk of megalomaniacs. People who let power go to their heads. Who, swayed by the siren song of sovereignty, ignored reason and wisdom. She had been witness to such power not so very long ago and, while not naive enough to believe all in the garden was rosy, she had dared to trust they had eliminated rule by domination.

"Apparently not," she muttered to herself. Her stomach knotted.

A confrontation would result in countless deaths, never mind that there were too few at the castello to mount more than a suicidal charge on Worthington.

Even if she mobilised the Hunters, who always relished a good skirmish, this would be tantamount to a war... one they had no hope of winning.

She sent up a prayer to her parents... *If ever I needed your tact, Papa, and your courage, Mama, now is the time.*

The city loomed larger. Its undulating outline — punctuated by the spectacular Duomo, assorted towers and churches, and the crenellations of the Palazzo Vecchio's Torre D'Arnolfo, although hazy under the smoke — evoked the glory of the Renaissance.

Sophia sucked in a breath, hoping such beauty was not ruined beyond repair.

"When you two have quite finished," she interrupted Angelo and Dario, who were still arguing. "If you have not yet come to an agreement, neither of you is suitable. I shall speak with Worthington."

This announcement was met with stunned gasps. Sophia's lack of diplomacy was legendary, even to Massimo and Aldo who had witnessed her bold rescue of Bianca and Gabriel from the hangman's noose.

"Y-you?" Angelo ventured, while Dario pressed his lips together to avoid tripping over his tongue.

"I," she replied imperiously.

"Use this." Dario, aware there was no budging Sophia when she dug in her heels, rifled in his satchel, and withdrew something bound by a thin strip of red silk. "Can't hurt." His face, the picture of innocence... a bad sign if ever there was one.

The others watched with avid interest as Sophia untied the ribbon and unrolled the sheet of parchment.

It appeared to be a letter of introduction from Callixtus to Worthington. The flowery yet formal language implying the bearer had the confidence of the chancellor and could be trusted to act on his behalf. That a truce was in the best interest of the City Dwellers in order to contain any threat of rebellion from outsiders. That strength was in unity not discord.

To ensure credibility, there was a scrawled signature at the bottom of the page alongside Callixtus' official seal.

Sophia was pleased to note the Hunters were not mentioned by name, but something was off, not least the timing.

She waved the sheet at Dario, eyeing him suspiciously. "When did his majesty write this, and why did he not simply give it to me before we left?"

A deep red stain crept up Dario's cheeks.

"You sneaky bugger." Angelo slapped his thigh and sniggered. "*You* wrote this."

Dario bowed.

Sophia's jaw dropped. "You are a man of hidden talents, Dario. This forgery is masterful, but Lordy, will you cop it when he finds out. Good job he loves you."

"Needs must when the devil drives." Dario grinned and did not rise to the bait. "Never mind the how's and when's, this will get us an audience with the prick, which is the whole point of the exercise. Now quit dallying."

13

The band arrived at the makeshift barrier — which marked the official egress from the city onto the southern road — under a white flag, carried by one of the Roman soldiers.

Although neither of the preening males squabbling over who was more suited to being the voice of the group had come to an accord on that particular topic, they *did* agree it would be unsightly for a Hunter to appear before *anyone* carrying a symbol of surrender, while seeking an audience.

Sophia whispered to Angelo, "Where is everyone? I can see only that one man leaving his guardhouse. Where is the rest of the patrol? Does Worthington actually imagine a single soldier is mighty enough to halt *us* never mind an invasion from the Romans?"

Putting her hand on the rail, Sophia shook it, steadying it quickly when it threatened to topple. Raising her voice, she brooded, "Not much of an obstacle. This *was* the city Nicoletta and Dante infiltrated, yes?" not wholly in jest.

She received nothing but puzzled shrugs in reply.

Sophia weighed up the scene, mulling over whether

Worthington had realised expending his assets to prevent an exodus was counterproductive, *or was the meagre welcoming committee a trick?*

At the lack of manpower ready to pounce on the unwary, she recalled what Nicoletta had said about Worthington ruling by menaces.

"Shame," Angelo growled almost inaudibly. "A good dust up would loosen the muscles before we confront the madman."

Reaching his side of the obstruction, the sentry stared down his nose at the riffraff in front of him. "What business do you have in Florence?"

All eyes turned to the Hunters' leader who thrust the forged document into the guard's face, and announced, "Inform the monsignor that Sophia Ricci, the Padrona of Upper Lazio and all of Umbria, is here to meet with him, and I bring tidings from the chancellor of Rome."

Despite the fact, the area over which Sophia claimed dominion only fell under the Hunters' control because the absence of humanity meant there was no one to issue a challenge, it did sound impressive. It harked back to when Sophia's father had instilled the military imperative of confidence when facing the enemy, into his daughters.

The man swung a nervous gaze between the woman and the note in her outstretched hand. He knew how quickly Worthington's temper escalated if he was interrupted for no good reason and had witnessed more than one bearer of bad tidings being relieved of his life.

Losing her patience, Sophia withdrew her sword and jabbed it at the guard. "Listen, you whelp, either fetch your master this moment or I'll run you through and present your disrespectful head to him myself."

Caught between a rock and a hard place, the poor guard opted for the lesser of two evils and scarpered.

The blade had whizzed too close for comfort, and he had no doubt she would execute her threat… gulping at his turn of thought, which extended as he ran.

Do I actually need to inform the monsignor, or can I simply vanish into the maze of streets and escape this rat-infested hellhole after nightfall?

The missive.

He slowed his pace.

The padrona of the Hunters — an infamous band of villains, so the tales went and supposedly equal to the monsignor's personal guard — was asking for a meeting and carried a document from the chancellor.

He came to a halt.

Worthington's plan to reign supreme over Italy required submission from the Roman Dwellers, and it dawned on the guard that what he did now could affect his leader's ambition… *if I garner a bounty in reward for using my initiative, that's merely a bonus.*

A humourless smile curved his mouth.

Better to have the letter and its deliverer with me than risk Worthington's wrath.

The lunatic could vent his spleen on the strangers, instead of his loyal guard.

Spinning on his heel, he retraced his steps to the checkpoint where the visitors loitered restlessly.

"My apologies, I forgot my manners. Please accompany me to the Palazzo, and I shall ask Monsignor Worthington whether he will grant you an audience."

The pompous figure lounging in a chair as overstuffed as its occupant's ego was slow to rise to greet the group being escorted into the grand room. A steely gaze bore into the guard, whose dreams of riches withered faster than the razed vines.

Disdainfully, Worthington studied his *guests*.

He sized up the two women: one standing a deferential pace behind the other.

Were these the fabled sisters of Middle Italy?

Their features were markedly dissimilar. His lip curled, as he recalled tales of the Hunters' immorality.

Doubtless their whore of a mother bedded more than one partner. I shall nip this rampant promiscuity in the bud once I have subdued the opposition and assumed the mantle of emperor.

Not the time, Carlyle, common sense contested. *Patience is an overrated virtue,* self-righteous zeal rebutted.

Reluctantly, Worthington coaxed his mind from the delights of oppressing the sinful to the issue at hand. As much as he hated abasing himself to speak to, let alone negotiate with, women, when it came to this group, he had no choice.

Breaking the uncomfortable silence, Worthington addressed Julia, assuming, because she appeared older and, thus, better educated than her companion, to be the aforementioned padrona.

Ignoring traditional pleasantries, he said, in a tone which conveyed the exact opposite, "I am delighted to make your acquaintance, Padrona Ricci. Allow me to welcome you to my city."

His, "I understand you have come—" was waved off by Julia, who indicated the other woman.

Swallowing a long-suffering sigh, the monsignor's attention slid to Sophia.

Before he could correct himself, Sophia — bristling with annoyance at his impertinence, inadvertent or otherwise — chided, "*Your city?* A curious assertion given the chancellor of Rome is hosting a woman whose proprietary rights over Florence and its surroundings pre-dates yours and who, I doubt, looking at how poorly the vineyards have been tended in her absence, will be happy with your stewardship."

Forcing a hearty chuckle, Worthington attempted to solidify his claim to the city. "Come now, my dear Padrona, we both know land rights are fleeting and, in the times we currently find ourselves, the weak do not deserve the privilege.

"Let us not squabble over inconsequential drivel. I understand you come with tidings from the aforementioned chancellor."

Worthington steepled his fingers and tapped his chin, contemplatively. "I confess, I find it unbecoming that the daughter of the great Noemi Ricci deems it appropriate to act as another's messenger… especially that of a Dweller." Disgruntled when the woman did not shrink at his admonishment.

Sophia squared her shoulders and lifted her chin, declaring proudly, to Angelo's chagrin, "I am honoured you are at least conversant enough with the rules of etiquette to respect the prior padrona of my people.

"I may be here on behalf of my clan," she took a step closer to Worthington, "but that same padrona raised me not to be subservient to any other human.

"I present you this…" Sophia dropped the letter on the table next to Worthington's chair, relieving her of the indignation of handing it to him. "…as a personal favour to a level-headed compatriot, who *also* feels war amongst us is a senseless waste of lives and resources.

"I am wearied from my travels and need to take a load off," she sank into the seat opposite Worthington, "while you read."

Without waiting for Worthington's permission, Sophia made herself comfortable.

Unable to come up with a pithy retort, Worthington made do with a shrug, put on a pair of glasses, and unrolled the parchment, whose innocuous contents revealed nothing more than Worthington would expect if the boot was on the other foot.

Greetings Monsignor,

I wish to express my appreciation for allowing my fellow leader safe entrance into Florence.

It is our abiding wish that we are able to orchestrate a mutually beneficial arrangement for the peaceful and prosperous future of our respective territories...

Bored with the blather, Worthington turned the page noting the signature, and a seal, which he surmised to be the man's personal cypher.

He reviewed the message, arriving at two conclusions. If the missive was genuine, it was imperative he, Worthington, removed the one called Callixtus from power for being an ineffectual dullard.

If his hunch proved correct and the letter was a cheap fraud, these damn Hunters were similarly deficient and, as should have happened at the outbreak, be exterminated before they could saddle a new generation with their *unique genetics*.

In either case, he decided to hold his cards close to his chest and play along with their charade.

Folding the letter, he set both it and his glasses on the table and walked to a bureau standing against the far wall.

He picked up a framed photograph and studied it briefly. "Tell me, Padrona," Worthington took great care to inject a modicum of civility in his voice. "What do you know of the world before its collapse?"

The question floored Sophia. She had no idea how this related to the topic at hand, but answered equably, "I was only a baby when it happened, but, occasionally while I was growing up, I overheard the camp elders discussing life before the pandemic. That it was an unimaginable misery which brought the world to its knees, and how hard the pharmaceutical companies, especially the one for whom Mama worked, battled to find a cure to stem the infection, but time ran out.

"Mama taught us about life prior to the devastation. I might not have lived it, but I am not ignorant." Her chin went up in warning that he was treading on shaky ground.

Worthington handed her the picture and resumed his seat.

Confused, she inspected the people in the image, registering that they all wore identical white laboratory coats, while using the time to concoct a satisfactory response.

Squinting at the figures, Sophia dug her nails into the wooden arm of the chair. Smiling at the camera, her mother. Next to her, taller than anyone else on the front row, an awkward-looking Carlyle Worthington.

The awareness that Worthington possessed information about her mother, set Sophia's teeth on edge. Her mind whirled as a raft of questions battled for answers only Noemi could provide. She fought to mask the uproar in her head.

Worthington grinned. "See a familiar face?"

"One. You," Sophia equivocated airily, determined not to let him see he was getting under her skin. "I am guessing the rest are fellow researchers. I did not take you for a scientist. I apologise for my misconceptions."

"No harm done, Padrona. As a businessman, my only interest in science was how it could benefit me financially."

He was impressed by how glibly the girl had sidestepped the truth, knowing full well she had recognised her mother. Thirty years ago, Noemi Ricci was the Director of Research for one of Worthington's Italian-based pharmaceutical subsidiaries, answerable to him alone.

"I do not know what influence ancient history has on today's conclave."

"You are wise for your age," Worthington's remark dripped with condescension. "Most would prattle on about how everyone needs to learn the lessons of the past. Yet, we know the past is just that and will never return."

Accepting his ploy had failed to garner the reaction he hoped for, he was about to change the subject when one of his men appeared.

The message delivered in hushed tones elicited a broad smile under his grizzled bread, and he instructed the young man, "See to it all is made ready."

The man saluted and exited the room without so much as a glance at the guests.

"May I beg your indulgence regarding the ancients before we bore ourselves with the drudgery of land grabs to carve up the peninsula."

"Meaning?"

"Food and libations in my private box in the Artemio Franchi Stadium. While it may not hold the historical worth of Rome's Flavian Amphitheatre, or its once majestic but, sadly lost, Florentine equivalent… something I hope to resurrect one day… I can assure you, it is worth the short trip."

The cogs in Sophia's brain were spinning. She did not want to share anything with this lunatic, least of all food, but how to decline without being discourteous? The new mother card… that ought to suffice.

"Your thoughtfulness is duly noted, Monsignor Worthington however, regrettably, I must decline." She paused delicately. "As a nursing mother, I must be vigilant. I am sure you, a man of the world, understands."

"I was informed of your condition, Padrona Ricci, and the drinks which await us will not affect your motherly duties adversely. You and your chancellor friend are not the only ones with spies at their disposal."

14

Unlike the rest of Florence, the Artemio Franchi Stadium had been painstakingly restored to its former glory as a world class football stadium, with the exception of the turf. That had been removed in favour of a gladiatorial arena.

In Worthington's skybox, Dario stood at the huge floor-to-ceiling window, regarding the vast circle of sand below. *Why bring them here? The man was a snake. What dastardly plot did he have up his sleeve?* He was gripped by a sense of foreboding, but experience told him to maintain an impassive demeanour. *Don't show any weakness.*

True to his word, Worthington had supplied a veritable feast, set out by his servants on a long buffet table. The fare appealed not only to those who had accompanied Sophia, but also to the padrona herself.

None was foolish enough to be the first to partake, concerned the food and drink contained more than a flavourful taste.

Seeing his guests hesitate, Worthington shook his head,

and filled his plate. "If I was planning something nefarious, it would not be with this bounty. Please, eat."

Sophia stepped forwards, to be prevented from sampling the repast by the Roman guards. Not in disrespect of the Hunter, but to serve as her food testers.

While, overtly, to protect a one-time sworn enemy, seemed a magnanimous gesture on their part, in truth, neither Massimo nor Aldo expected to survive until day's end, and preferred to face their demise on a full stomach.

To their surprise, the spread was delicious and safe to eat. After weeks of field rations, the pair piled their plates high, wolfing down mouthfuls as though starved, until Dario cleared his throat.

"Satisfied?" Worthington's tone was silky, but his expression remained bland.

Sophia did not respond, instead she skirted Dario's men, to peruse the delights on offer.

Reaching the selection of drinks at the end of the table, Sophia found her host had indeed considered her condition as a new mother, providing a couple of steins of dark aromatic stout, its benefits eulogised in old wives' tales.

How the hell does a man like Worthington know? Unable to answer her own question, she pushed it to the back of her mind, and joined him in the cushioned chairs.

Speaking around a slice of prosciutto Toscano, Worthington sought to quell the curiosity which had nagged at him since he had shown the girl the picture.

"Sophia. May I call you Sophia? We can consider it a step towards mutual cooperation."

Nibbling on a square of delectable chocolate, Sophia rolled her eyes internally, but managed to smile and nod.

"Why did you conceal a truth from me?"

She stopped mid-chew and quirked a quizzical brow at him, as though unsure to what he alluded.

Levelling his penetrating gaze at her, he elaborated, "The photograph. You recognised your mother standing next to me. I daresay her death was not so long ago that you have forgotten what she looked like."

The clang of steel against steel jerked Sophia's attention to the arena floor where two men, clad in nothing but loincloths emblazoned with the snarling head of a lion, battled one another in an apparent duel to the death.

Both were drenched in sweat from the heat of the day, chests laced with gashes from the bites of their blades, the sands darkening with their blood.

Her eyes fixed on the clash below the window, Sophia replied, "If you knew my mother was in the picture, why did you bother to ask?"

"Because, as I said before, I am curious as to how much you know of the past?"

"Do not play games with me, Worthington…"

"Are we back to formalities?"

"…you have an ulterior motive behind your question. Stop beating about the bush, and just say it."

"As you wish." Worthington dipped his head.

The conversation paused as the match between the soldiers came to its inevitable conclusion with the death of one at the hands of the other.

The winner saluted the box before limping off, his opponent dragged from the battle ground. A spectacle repeated by two more combatants, similarly attired.

"You must be cognisant of your mother's duplicity at the end of civilisation?"

This wrested Sophia's gaze back to Worthington. "Are you out of your mind? My mother struggled day and night trying to curb the spread of the disease—"

Worthington guffawed at his guest's naïveté. "Did she fail to tell you she was employed by the corporation who developed the virus which wiped out seventy-five percent of the population? It was her team's responsibility to save the world. They failed."

Sophia blanched at his words, turning slightly so her host did not see the tears swimming in her eyes, only to witness another man perish in the sands.

"Why? Why commit such an horrendous crime against humanity?" she asked, her voice dropping to a whisper, unsure whether she was asking her mother or Worthington.

Worthington glowered. "I told you, I am a businessman, and science was conquering major maladies. That's not good for profits. I concede, even I was not prepared for the outcome. Then again, what is the saying? 'When one door closes, another opens'. Being ruler of the world is far preferable to having unlimited wealth."

The next duel was about to commence. The combatants served up to the unwitting audience by a posse of spear-wielding soldiers. The ill-fated participants had no escape.

This bout pitted a man carrying a net, a dagger and what appeared to be some kind of a trident, against an opponent armed with a rectangular shield and a vicious-looking sword.

Stunned into silence, Worthington's guests stared at the man holding the net, recognising his stance and the distinguishing scars etched into his body, with scarcely concealed horror.

It was none other than Dante.

"A demonstration of what one might expect to enjoy once my amphitheatre is reconstructed," Worthington's tone was almost dreamy.

Shards of ice skittered down Sophia's spine. The man was taken by madness. To kill in defence of your lands and your life was one thing. To force men to kill for entertainment was quite another.

She studied the combatants. Helmet-less, Dante's only protection was a padded guard, on his left arm and a metal shoulder protector.

His adversary also sported metal guards, one on his right arm and the other on his left leg, both held in place by leather strips *but,* he had a helmet, albeit with small eyeholes to prevent being jabbed by the trident, and flanges shaped like fish fins to protect his neck.

Dante would have to rely on agility and speed to outwit his foe.

"The Retiarius versus the Secutor," Worthington announced. "The fisherman versus the fish," he clarified at the baffled faces surrounding him. "Tsk, and you consider yourselves well-versed in history. For shame."

Glancing at the sands, Worthington spat, "Consider yourself luckier than your friend down there. At least I was generous enough to wine and dine you before feeding you to *my* lions.

"Would you believe he had the balls to sneak into my city a second time, using your arrival as cover. My guards said he spouted some nonsense about wreaking vengeance on me for harming his mate. A real man would not allow that to happen in the first place.

"And as for you, *girl.*" Worthington narrowed his eyes at Sophia. "Your mother is not around to save your worthless ass as she did when she fled my laboratories with an untested vaccine. Hmmm, maybe I should amend that. One she had tested on herself and, presumably, given you survived the pandemic, eventually on you and your sister."

Below, the two men circled each other, prowling like wild beasts, choosing the opportune moment to strike.

At the same moment they launched their attack, a group of Worthington's men burst into the skybox.

Daring to interrupt, the leader exclaimed, "Sir, there is a column of militia assembling outside our southern gate."

Worthington got to his feet. "Why are you badgering me about so insignificant a matter? Order the troops to dispatch the intruders."

"B-But, Monsignor, they have weaponised vehicles comparable with ours, bearing the insignia of Rome."

Dario breathed, "And not a moment too soon."

Only Sophia heard the comment, and prudence dictated she ought not to react.

Worthington was too busy barking orders to bother with others in the room.

Pushing by the patrol, he glared at Sophia. "I must take my leave. Seems I am to be blessed with yet more uninvited company, something I am sure you know nothing about." He twisted to address his sergeant.

"If any of these intruders so much as twitch, kill them with extreme prejudice."

"Aye, Monsignor."

As inexorably as the door swung closed, Sophia's gaze was drawn back to the sands.

Time slowed to a standstill.

How can I explain Dante's death to Nic? Sophia's anguish was arrested when she saw, to her astonishment, the wounded Hunter astride the now unhelmeted gladiator, raining vicious blows to the man's face.

In a flash, Dante switched from his hands to the helmet, smashing it against his adversary's head.

Beside them on the ground, the Secutor's sword lay tangled in the net.

The soldier defeated, Sophia beseeched, even though she knew Dante could not hear, "You won, do not tarry. Get your butt back to the castello and your wife, who will likely slap you senseless, not only for your recklessness, but also for leaving her behind."

A commotion erupted behind her. She became aware of the drum of boots as Dario and his guards, swords drawn, charged Worthington's men.

The clash was fierce.

The thump of bodies hitting the floor filled the skybox but, despite the melee... and imminent danger... Sophia was strangely detached, trying to equate the mother she knew with the person Worthington had described and coming up with a big fat blank.

Was Mama responsible for the devastating contagion?

Her momentary distraction left her at a disadvantage, exacerbated when, cornered next to the huge window, she spotted Worthington's sergeant bearing down on her, his dagger poised. Simultaneously, she caught the glint of another knife — more specifically, a surgical scalpel.

Expertly, Julia slit the man's carotid artery, while Angelo protected the medic's back from the advance of two Bolognese soldiers.

The blood from the attack sprayed Sophia.

To see the physician act as a Hunter impressed the padrona and, being bathed in the sergeant's warm blood, triggered a savagery Sophia had not felt since saving her sister in Rome. *Bianca... Worthington's assertion was something they needed to discuss when this debacle was over.*

The brush with death honed her wits and, setting aside what she could not rectify, Sophia acted on instinct. A knife and fork her only weapons, she eviscerated anyone she did not recognise.

Dario hefted one of Worthington's troopers, who had met his fate at the end of Sophia's fury and tossed him through the window.

Dante looked up at the sound of shattering glass to see

Dario pointing in his direction and commanding Julia to tend to him.

He would have to wait. There was no time for healing.

The remaining guerillas positioned around the stadium flooded onto the sand. Grabbing the net and the sword, Dante faced the onslaught.

Sophia joined Julia and Dario at the broken window, seeing the guards converge on Dante.

"Dario, save your brother. Julia, stay with me, you are no good to them dead."

"Begging your pardon, Padrona, but like hell I will. I am a fighter first and a medic second. Dante needs us both."

Taken aback by Julia's vehemence, Sophia was at a loss, until the former clarified, "Bianca's training extended way beyond medicine. Let me prove myself to both of you."

Gripping her scalpel, Julia started for the window without waiting for permission, to be stopped by Sophia who snagged Angelo's sword.

"This was my present to him on our wedding night. It is yours now, make me proud."

Julia hugged Sophia. "Aye, my Padrona."

Tossing a wordless *thank you* to her sister for her foresight, Sophia felt a warm glow infuse her being at Julia's avowal, happy to welcome the medic into her tribe.

She watched the pair charge down the grandstands into the fray. Turning to her husband, she picked up two discarded blades, and handed one to him.

A frown marred his forehead, "Thanks sweetheart, but I prefer the one you gave away."

"Suck it up, my love. I'll get you another."

"Promises, promises," he scoffed, as he opened the door, following it up with, "Shall we?"

Massimo and Aldo, faces grim, blades dripping with

blood, brought up the rear as Sophia and Angelo began their search for Worthington.

15

Following the incursion by the Hunters five years previously, and unbeknownst to the majority of Rome's citizens, Callixtus had made it a priority to scour the numerous abandoned service stations in and around the sprawling city — specifically their vast and reinforced underground storage reservoirs.

Unobtrusively, he set about restoring the once defunct Torrevaldaliga Nord power station, then tasked a select group of trusted scientists and engineers to formulate a viable fuel. His aim, to power not only the city in the not-too-distant future, but also… and more immediately… their small fleet of Leopard 2 tanks.

The success of the venture was evidenced by the arrival, under Callixtus' direction, of the Roman Armoured Legion which had captured the southern portion of the city and were making a push to the north.

The chancellor had ordered his men to spare Florence, if possible, but to level it if necessary. Thus far, the course of the battle did not bode well for the survival of the ancient city.

Worthington's snipers had stationed themselves in any church belfry or tower they could wedge themselves into, desperately trying to check the invasion.

Leaden hail and rocket propelled grenades rained down from above but, by the time Worthington had rallied his mechanised battalion to the centre of Florence, the columns of Roman tanks were already there.

While a head-on confrontation in the generously proportioned city squares meant Callixtus made speedy progress, the unwieldy tanks ground to a painful halt when the open spaces gave way to the narrow twists and turns of medieval streets.

History repeated itself as roads became the greatest enemy to both sides, and the motorised battle morphed into dogged, hand-to-hand combat.

Advancing yard by yard, the Roman troops exploited whatever shelter was available to stave off each attack; the dead and dying not spared the indignity of their bodies being used as shields for the living.

Despite being thinly spread, the small cohort of Hunters was also inflicting serious damage on their adversaries, cutting a swath through what seemed to be an unceasing wave of Worthington's men.

In the arena, Dario and Julia reached Dante. Backs to each other, they positioned themselves in a loose triangle to deflect the advance. The skirmish was fierce but, even with Dante's berserker rage, it did not require a mathematical genius to recognise they were outnumbered ten to one.

Just when they expected to be cut down, a deafening blare from what must have been an enormous horn had a startling effect on their attackers. As one they turned and bolted from the arena.

Dante, his ears ringing, spat on his blade and twirled it casually; his outward nonchalance belied by the tremble in his hand. "Something we said?"

"No idea, but that horn can't be good news for us," Dario rasped as he sucked in a lungful of air, letting the tip of his sword dip to the ground so he could lean on the hilt. "Hell's teeth, I am out of practice."

"Injuries?" Ever the medic, Julia ran an experienced eye over her fellow combatants, satisfied they had suffered nothing more than a few cuts and scrapes. "How you avoided that Secutor…" She did not finish her sentence, shaking her head at Dante's sheer dumb luck. "The Gods definitely favoured you."

Breath caught, Dario in the lead, and praying they did not get lost in the maze of corridors, the three took off in hot pursuit.

It was not hard to track their quarry whose voices echoed off the walls. Mindful they could be running into a trap, Dario lifted his arm to slow their mad dash as they reached the main exit. Cracking the door ajar, he peered out, the bright sunlight making him squint after the dim interior.

Nobody to be seen. Not a guard, not a soldier, not a single person.

It was ominously quiet.

Confused, Dario edged out and flattened himself against the building, scanning left and right. "Where the bloody hell is everyone?"

Dante and Julia followed, shading their eyes against the glare.

Aware they were wasting precious seconds, Dario knew they would waste even more if they went the wrong way, and turned to his brother. "Does Worthington have an HQ?"

Dante's brows knitted. "Not a clue. That was the one thing we were unable to discover..." he paused, something teased at his subconscious. A graphic tale narrated by the doomed Condottiero Glorioso of Florence, briefing them on his unceremonious flight. "...but I'd wager it's the Palazzo Vecchio."

The same palace where the monsignor had hosted the Hunters. Dario kicked himself for not taking note of the route.

"Why there?"

"According to Luca and Sienna, it's a great vantage point. High tower overlooking the river and the city. Plus, there's a secret passage which takes you right across the Ponte Vecchio to the Pitti Palace. Perfect for a quick escape."

"Ok, we'll head that way. Hopefully we'll come across Angelo and Sophia. You know this city." Dario waved a hand at Dante. "Onwards James and don't spare the horses."

Julia, who happened to know this centuries-old saying, chided. "You need to get out more," adding in an aside to Dante, "and it's 'Home James', but don't ask."

"Wasn't going to." Dante grinned then, turning left onto the Viale Manfredo Fanti 2, set a gruelling pace along the cracked pavements, over a decaying iron bridge which crossed the once busy but sadly long disused railway, leading them unerringly towards the heart of Florence.

Meanwhile, Sophia, Angelo, and the two guards had come upon Callixtus who greeted them with an exultant beam. Antonio, acting as the chancellor's protection detail in Dario's absence, heard familiar voices, and climbed out of the turret, giving vent to a loud whoop at the sight of his brother and Sophia.

"We will quash these piddling insects by nightfall," Callixtus proclaimed. "They are surrendering left right and centre. Apparently being taken prisoner is preferable to being handed over to the populace."

Sophia chuckled. "But you haven't seen his eminence?"

"Neither hide nor hair."

"We think he'll go to ground in the palazzo where we met him. It's not far from the river. Huge tower."

"Want a lift?"

"Thought you'd never ask."

Callixtus reached down to haul Sophia onto the tank; Antonio doing the same for Angelo. The twins slapped each other on the back.

"Where's Dario and co?" Antonio cast an eye over the crowd. No sign of the other three.

"Rescuing Dante. Long story," Angelo replied.

"Julia too?" Antonio's quick question was too casual, prompting Angelo to shoot him a thoughtful glance.

"Julia too. Why?"

"Mind your beeswax."

Not known for his tact, Angelo held his brother's gaze for long seconds, then nodded knowingly and, for once, did not press the issue.

Given the armoured vehicle would struggle to manage a slow trot, Massimo and Aldo opted to walk behind.

Sophia stretched out and leant against the rounded gun turret. "Bliss."

"I think you and I need to have a chat about what constitutes 'bliss'," Angelo teased.

"Yeah, yeah." She flapped her hand at him.

No time for banter, the couple updated Callixtus on recent events. "He needs to be stopped, and today," Sophia concluded. "We cannot allow him to escape this city. If he does, he will simply begin again, along with any of his cronies who avoid capture."

"Like every other despot, there are those who relish in dishing out extreme punishment. They are the dangerous ones, these other poor schmucks are nothing but cannon fodder," Angelo opined.

"Do you know, he organised gladiatorial games for our *entertainment*?" Sophia's voice rose a notch in her indignation. "He even dared send one of my men... *my men* into the arena, presumably expecting him to be killed... right in front of our eyes. Ohhh, death is too good for him."

Angelo caught her eye, seeing his own anger reflected there. "We'll get him."

Not far away, an intrepid trio was making rapid progress across Florence. Curiously, their way was unhindered by Worthington's forces. Not prepared to assume Callixtus and his legions had taken the city, the closer they got to the palazzo the more likely it seemed that the chancellor had triumphed.

"Worthington's a slippery snake," Dante warned. "It would be a mistake to rest on our laurels."

"Duly noted," Dario replied.

The clatter of hooves shattered the uneasy silence and sent them darting into a narrow side street.

"Dante Barzetti, stop lurking in that alley, and get your sorry ass out here this instant," an infuriated woman's voice demanded.

Julia and Dario stared at Dante who flushed bright red.

"I do believe those are the dulcet tones of your mate."

Dario gave a wolfish grin. "Time to face the music." He shoved his brother. "Go, deal with Nic. We'll meet you at the palazzo." He swaggered out of the alley, tipped his head at the figure who had dismounted. "Nic."

"Don't you 'Nic' me," Nicoletta hissed. "You're both as bad as each other."

"Hey, I did not know his plans." Dario raised his palms in a conciliatory fashion.

"Your leg," Julia wailed.

"Do not fret, Dweller. My leg can suffer a horse ride," Nicoletta retorted.

"It's not the horse ride I'm worried about," Julia muttered, but allowed Dario to usher her along the street. "Just promise me you'll be careful," she threw over her shoulder.

Nicoletta hobbled awkwardly to where Dante waited… somewhat nervously it must be admitted. His wife had taken secreting deadly weapons about her person to a fine art.

The sharp slap resounded around the empty neighbourhood. "You bloody fool. What the *hell* were you thinking? Were you even thinking at all? I cannot be mother and father to our children. Do you *want* my heart to break?"

Slightly stunned, Dante opened his mouth to defend his actions.

Nicoletta's hand shot up. "Do not dare. Nothing you say can justify disappearing without telling me." The palm cracked against his cheek a second time, followed by fists pummelling his chest. "Have you any idea…" her shoulders heaved, and the next moment she was in his arms.

"Sorry, love. I let my anger at Worthington override my common sense." His quiet apology doing more than anything to placate his wife.

"Do not let it happen again but, should temptation beckon, don't leave me behind." Nicoletta sniffed and swallowed her sobs. "Right, time to get the bastard." Her injury no hindrance, she mounted the huge black stallion, helping Dante up behind her.

Not sure whether his mate was more affronted that he left without telling her, or because he didn't include her, Dante chose not to ask and made do with sneaking a kiss on her nape.

"It's a bloody good job I love you." She leant into him, then clicked her heels, spurring the horse towards the Piazza della Signoria, the square which was home to the Palazzo Vecchio.

16

The sun was beginning its slow downwards journey by the time the massed armies of Rome, augmented by the Hunters, had filled the streets of Florence, squashing the last pockets of resistance. The battalion of tanks had cut a remorseless path through the machines of the Bolognese.

Contrary to the usual wave of jubilation, the atmosphere was subdued.

Their victory, although unequivocal, was not celebrated.

Too many lives had been forfeited… on both sides.

A city ravaged because of one man's ego.

Incredibly, and in no small thanks to Callixtus' orders, a remarkable number of buildings had survived the wanton destruction levied by Worthington's troops, who seemed to be working under the premise that if they couldn't have the city, no one would.

Any of those enslaved citizens, now freed from their oppressors, who were able had joined their compatriots from the south, currently congregating in the Piazza della Signoria.

The rest were being treated, under Bianca's supervision, in one of the encampments on the perimeter of the city which, by its very position, had avoided the worst of the offensive.

Sophia, perched on the nose of the chancellor's tank, stared up at the imposing palazzo where they assumed Worthington had taken refuge.

Detailed intel about the interior was essential otherwise they could be caught unawares, especially as they had no clue how many men were protecting Worthington. The only people with that knowledge were dead or in Rome. *Dammit.*

Their best chance lay with the two who had infiltrated the city. *Had they garnered anything useful?* "Where are Nic and Dante when you need them," she grumbled out loud.

"Right here," a cheerful voice chirped.

Sophia twisted in the direction of the speaker, a broad grin warming her face at the sight of her Security Chief with her mate, the latter relatively unscathed, and a massive stallion. "You two just hate missing out, dontcha." She slithered off the tank to draw Nicoletta into a hug.

"Well, someone has to keep an eye on you rabble. Clearly, you are a magnet for danger," Nicoletta countered dryly, handing the reins to a capable-looking soldier.

"Oh, ha bloody ha." Sophia stuck out her tongue. "Talking about rabble, where are Dario and Julia?"

"We thought they would be here. They were ahead of us. Dante and I had a discussion to conclude." Nicoletta's droll expression required no clarification.

Sophia chuckled. "Called it." She beckoned to Angelo and Callixtus, then fixed an urgent gaze on Nicoletta. "I know you haven't actually been inside, but can you tell us anything about this palazzo? I want that man's head on my wall."

"Awww, don't we get first dibs?" Dante objected. "He shot my wife."

"We can argue dibs later. We hardly saw more than the entrance. Worthington's reception room was on the ground floor, and I don't want to be fossicking around an old building in the dark. Spill."

Dredging through her brain for Luca's vivid recitation of Worthington's incursion and the subsequent attack in the great hall of the palazzo, as well as what she had gleaned from questioning those locals prepared to speak, Nicoletta was able to provide a workable description, while Dante sketched a crude map in the dust coating the armoured vehicle.

"He'll risk the hidden corridor, Luca told us about," Dante said. "He thinks his gladiator bested me, that Nicoletta is already dead, or at least incapacitated, and assumes no one else among his enemies knows of the passage."

"How do we find it?"

"We know it's on one of the upper floors, other than that… on a wing and a prayer," Dante shrugged, "but we gotta try." He turned to lead the way, only to be hailed from the crowd.

"Oi, wait for us."

Dario and Julia appeared, looking slightly dishevelled but determined.

Dante hugged his brother. "Where'd you get to?"

"A band of Worthington's men deemed it their duty to delay us. We rectified their opinion."

Julia grinned. "I really should not enjoy making work for myself, but I cannot deny it was fun." Her gaze slid to Antonio, and a silent message passed between them, which everyone saw but no one commented on.

"No work if they're dead," Dante chipped in, to nods all around.

"Dear lord, we've created a monster." Sophia shook her head. "Come on, let's do this."

Callixtus gave orders to a detachment of his men to bring up the rear. Then, once they were inside the palazzo, to spread out and disperse… in whatever manner they chose… any of Worthington's stragglers.

This time, they would not be taking prisoners.

Sophia's posse, including Massimo and Aldo who relished the notion of a good hunt, faced no opposition as they marched into the palazzo. It was oddly quiet. Dust motes danced in the dying rays of the setting sun glimmering through myriad windows.

On silent feet and swords drawn, soldiers scattered to do their commander's bidding. An occasional and quickly muffled scream the only indication they were locating their prey.

Torches guttering in wall sconces did little to alleviate the increasing gloom, but there was light enough to see as Dante led them through the ancient building in search of the map room, retracing their steps several times when they took a wrong turn.

Despite the urgency of their task, the group slowed as they crossed a vast hall, mesmerised by its breathtaking murals. Not even the streaks of dried blood, the only evidence of Worthington's unprovoked assault, detracted from their magnificence.

"Such skill." Sophia tilted her head, unable to credit they were created by a human hand.

"A treat for another day." Angelo urged them onwards. "We have no time to linger."

Reluctantly, they followed Dante, but more than one among them kept looking back at the magnificent salon.

"It's called the Hall of the Five Hundred, so Sienna informed us," Nicoletta said as they hurried along another chilly passageway. "Apparently, this place is overflowing with mind-blowing artworks, which somehow withstood the end of civilisation. Those Renaissance artists really knew their stuff."

Classically educated, Callixtus refrained from emitting a pained groan at the term 'stuff' and, instead, concentrated on not falling behind the Hunters as they sped after Dante.

"Do you not think the dearth of defence is strange?" Sophia contested in guarded undertones.

"Our reputation precedes us." Angelo smirked.

"It's too easy. What if he's prepared an ambush?"

"Slow up, Dante," Callixtus ordered quietly. "Sophia's right. We are rushing in without a foolproof plan."

The group huddled together and thrashed out a reasonably effective strategy, which basically boiled down to, watch your back and try not to get killed.

Sophia knew how badly Dante wanted to confront Worthington but was concerned his fury would rob him of his usual cunning. That said, the man deserved his revenge, not to mention, he was their best chance of locating the secret passage.

"Dante and Angelo, you're with me. Nicoletta, take Antonio, Julia, and Dario, clear that section, then follow us." Sophia pointed to a door. "Callixtus, Massimo, and Aldo, check the tower. We don't want the zealot making a bid for martyrdom.

"If any of you dares to get killed, you will have Noemi to answer to, and that includes you four." She jabbed a finger at the Romans. "Trust me, you don't want to spend eternity placating that wraith for your carelessness.

"Everybody clear?"

Tacit assent came in the bob of nine heads and the three groups melted into the shadows.

Shortly thereafter, Dante, masking his relief, ushered Sophia and Angelo into a room of generous proportions, dominated by an enormous globe standing in the centre, and whose walls were adorned with numerous maps.

Despite obvious neglect, the exquisite maps, protected behind glass frames, looked as though they had been painted months, not centuries, ago.

"*Wow*." Sophia remembered to keep her voice low. "This is amazing."

The temptation to linger, to admire the beautiful cartography was almost too great. Unable to help herself, she stroked the globe, her slender fingers leaving long smears in the dust, revealing the glossy surface underneath.

"Whoever drew these was a genius." Sophia's eyes as wide as an inquisitive child's.

"We can come back," Angelo murmured, taking her hand.

Sophia smiled at him, knowing the probability of them surviving the encounter with Worthington was slim to unlikely, rendering his promise null and void, but loving his optimism. "I'll hold you to that." She lifted up on tiptoe to press a kiss to his lips.

"Save it for later, you two," Dante, who… by sheer fluke because he had forgotten it was Armenia he was looking for… had found the pertinent map, interrupted, all but hopping about in his impatience. "Lovely art, blah blah blah. For pity's sake, stop dallying."

Sophia rolled her eyes. "Geez, Dante, calm the farm. We're coming."

"You don't understand. If Worthington decided to escape this way, he got a significant head start on us, and could be across the river by now. We'll never catch him once he reaches the palace. There are too many variables."

"So… how?" Sophia's gaze circled the room. The only obvious exit was the door through which they had entered.

"Ta daaaaa." With a flourish, Dante bowed and swung open one of the maps.

Sophia and Angelo gaped.

"No way," they gasped in unison.

"Way." A smug smirk curving his mouth, Dante climbed into the hole behind the map and vanished.

"Wait up." Angelo darted back into the passage to grab a torch, then he and Sophia leapt after Dante.

Mirroring the flight of Luca, Sienna, and their escort, all those weeks… a lifetime… ago, the people prepared to lay their lives on the line to restore Florence to its rightful governor, raced along the Vasari corridor.

Over the bridge to the Uffizi Gallery, crossing the Lungarno dei Archibusieri, and tracking parallel with the River Arno to the Ponte Vecchio. The only sound, the rapid pad of running feet.

Panting at their breakneck pace, they reached the long gallery which spanned the Arno.

Ahead, half-way over the bridge, they spotted a group of about half a dozen men strolling leisurely, as though enjoying a Sunday promenade around a park, showing no sign of panic or haste.

"*Worthington.*"

Sophia's hiss barely broke the hush, but the man in question heard, and spun on his heel.

"You!" he snarled. "Why are you not dead?"

"Takes more than your pettifogging imbeciles to fell a Hunter," she sniped. "Time to face the music. Time to see whether your divine right to rule the world holds true."

"Sophia, you have a son who might like to get to know his mother. Sit this one out," Angelo exhorted.

Sophia faced him, her eyes spitting fire and something else — something primal, visceral. Angelo's heart thudded. This was the Sophia he had fallen in love with: the hellion, the warrior, impetuous, wilful, and fearless. Yes, she had softened over the past year or so, more so once she was pregnant, but he knew her wild spirit lurked like a restless panther waiting to pounce.

He had to let her do this.

"Go get him, *tesoro mio*. Claim his scalp."

"*Ti amo,* Angelo." Sophia blew him a kiss, as she brandished her sword. "If…"

He shook his head. "Not tonight… I got your back."

Sophia strode forwards, flanked by Dante and Angelo a step behind.

"Take them," Worthington barked. "She's mine."

Sophia snorted with mirth. "Haha, you are hilarious."

Her features hardened. "I am no one's." She pinned him with an implacable gaze. "Do you believe me?"

Worthington glared. "It will be my pleasure to prove you wrong.

"We'll see about that."

Oblivious to the brawl unfolding around them, Sophia and Worthington charged, coming together at the middle of the bridge, with the bone jarring impact of two battle tanks.

It was on!

In the confines of the corridor, steel against steel created spirals of sparks, illuminating the frenzied tableau in jagged bursts as though the adversaries were in the midst of a soundless storm.

Bitter memories of the days before the truce with Rome reared up, triggering the Hunters' once notorious homicidal rage. Mercilessly, Angelo and Dante slaughtered their foe with clinical indifference.

Chest heaving with effort, Dante prepared to skewer the last of them, but the slippery eel managed to dodge the slash of the sword and scarpered back the way they had come.

A shrill scream, cut off, suggested he had not made good his escape.

Now, there were two.

Angelo could see the sweat beading on Sophia's brow. He studied his wife; relieved to note her sword arm was not drooping, and her movements were not laboured. She was dancing on the balls of her feet, pirouetting around Worthington, who looked pale, his lips dry.

Still, it would not do to underestimate the man. "Watch him," he said under his breath to Dante. "He will not fight fair."

"Surely, as long as he dies, does it matter who wielded the death blow?" Dante muttered.

"This is a matter of honour for Sophia. He executed two of our own in cold blood, and tried to assassinate several more, including you and Nic. It is way beyond personal."

The duel showed no signs of ceasing. Neither opponent gave the other quarter, and false steps were punished with callous swiftness.

At some point the spectators grew from two to nine, bringing with them extra torches, which made the scene more rather than less macabre.

Nicoletta apprised the others of their success in rounding up assorted members of Worthington's administration. "Snivelling cowards, the lot of them," was her considered opinion.

The moon had risen in the crystal-clear sky, bathing the Ponte Vecchio in its ethereal glow, its soft beams doing little to brighten the improvised battlefield. A ghostly mist, a result of the rapidly cooling air, hovered just above the surface of the river, adding to the eerie atmosphere.

Catching a glimpse of the phenomena as she writhed sinuously, to deflect Worthington's increasingly wild lunges, Sophia taunted, "See, you pompous buffoon, even the river knows your rule was all smoke and mirrors. Naught but a mirage wrought by trickery and vacuous promises."

She parried his thrust, pivoting to face him with athletic prowess. It was difficult to imagine she had given birth mere weeks ago.

"Pah, what do you know of power?" Worthington scorned, slapping her blade aside. "The rabble *you* purport to rule have no loyalty, they will kill you, soon as look at you, and good riddance to bad rubbish."

Sophia howled with laughter. "At least their loyalty is not enforced, driven by intimidation or the desire to control."

"How long are we going to let this continue?" Callixtus' conversational tone gave no hint of his disquiet over the protracted encounter. "How are they not exhausted?"

"Until Sophia asks for help, or she is incapacitated," Angelo replied.

"You will allow him to wound her?" Julia was shocked.

"It's her call. Doesn't mean I like it. Given the chance, I would happily gut the cretin, but I gave my word."

At that precise moment, Sophia, dodging a particularly vicious jab, swung away only to be blinded by a shaft of moonlight. She stumbled, staggered backwards, and nearly fell.

Cursing, Angelo jumped to his feet, poised to intervene.

Worthington's maniacal laughter reverberated along the corridor. "Slain by a moonbeam. Pathetic child."

The slash of his blade lacerated Sophia's right arm from shoulder to elbow. Blood, black in the flicker of the torch, marred the ripped sleeve of her shirt, and oozed down to her fingers.

Her sword clattering to the tiled floor, Sophia dropped to one knee, gulping air into her aching lungs, her injured limb throbbing.

"You bastard," she growled. "I cannot sew, and I hate doing laundry."

Sensing victory, Worthington raised his sword.

A fatal error.

In a flash, Sophia whipped out the weapon sheathed to her to calf. Mustering up the last of her strength, she shrieked like a banshee, and shot upright. So quickly, no one saw the dagger gripped in both hands until it was embedded in the monsignor's belly.

Grunting with effort, she filleted her nemesis like a fish.

Astounded at his spectacular and wholly unexpected defeat, Worthington stared at the gruesome wound, his mouth opening and shutting impotently. He wheezed something unintelligible, frantically trying to prevent his innards spilling out.

Relieving him of his blade, Sophia leant close to a man already dead.

"Not quite divine, then," she scoffed.

Worthington's legs buckled, he reeled, clawing at the air in a desperate bid to stay upright.

Defeat was something he refused to countenance.

Fate… although royally pissed off that Worthington considered himself a god, took pity on him, and before shock gave way to agony… snatched his life.

Spent, Sophia repeated, less than lucidly, "See, smoke and mirrors."

Turning her back on Worthington, her exhausted gaze landed on Angelo who darted forwards as his mate swayed drunkenly.

"I've got you," he soothed, scooping her into his arms.

"I'm yours," Sophia whispered, and then, for the first time in her life… to her undying mortification, compounded by the fact it was witnessed by all and sundry who had no intention of letting her forget it… she fainted.

Smoke & Mirrors

EPILOGUE

In the aftermath of the emancipation of Florence, as the debacle became known, Callixtus delegated a garrison to track down and arrest the surviving members of Worthington's guard.

The Roman chancellor felt summary execution was too good for the scum — who had no compunction enslaving innocent citizens then working them to death — and meted out commensurate retribution.

Under penalty of being hung, drawn, and quartered if they put a toe, never mind a whole foot, out of line, Worthington's henchmen were tasked with restoring the city to its former glory, as well as regenerating the decimated fields.

Although Gabriel was in charge of the rebuilding program — an assignment Bianca took advantage of to establish a training program for burgeoning medics — and a contingent of trusted soldiers would monitor progress, the principal overseers were none other than the previously oppressed locals.

Karma was, most definitely, a bitch!

Sophia, the injury to her arm stitched by Bianca who was prone to wrap her sister in cotton wool, was persuaded to rest for several days before beginning the journey home.

Time alone with Angelo and Giulio, away from the pressures of being padrona of the oft recalcitrant Hunters, was an unexpected blessing.

Succumbing to her mate's cosseting while recuperating also served to revitalise and strengthen a relationship which had faced an assortment of hurdles in its brief existence, not least that Sophia had a tendency to treat Angelo as favoured pet rather than an adored partner.

To be fair, Angelo had proved himself a worthy mate, shouldering responsibility with the confidence of a seasoned professional — a world away from the streets of his childhood.

Protection of the Hunters' territory was safe in their hands.

Nicoletta and Dante returned to the encampment immediately. In the main to reunite with Zara and Rocco, but also to reassure the Hunters that war had been averted. News, which was received with varying degrees of relief, given the hotheads amongst them were spoiling for a good fight.

Needless to state, their respective mates were more than happy to spell out the error of such asinine reasoning.

Night after night, huddled around campfires, Nicoletta and Dante regaled those of their comrades who had stayed behind to protect the camp with tales of the confrontation and their own participation, which grew taller with every telling.

Accompanying the couple, Antonio and… to the shock of Dario and Callixtus, but no one else… Julia. Their relationship — kept under wraps at Julia's insistence because she didn't want to jeopardise her position or risk her training — revealed to their nearest and dearest in the days after the battle.

Sophia *was* heard to mutter that for two people claiming to be in love, Callixtus and Dario could be remarkably blind to the same in others, resulting in some good-hearted ribbing of the chancellor and his mate.

After thanking Callixtus for his hospitality and his sterling efforts to save her city, Sienna pledged to take better care of the citizens in Florence than had her late husband.

Although, latterly, Sienna had behaved less than graciously, she was honest enough to acknowledge that Luca had rescued her from a life of poverty.

Orphaned at birth, the midwife had sold Sienna to a rich family who treated her more like a servant than a daughter. Running away, she had found sanctuary among a troupe of dancers who took her in and was where, eventually, Luca spotted her, courted her and whisked her away.

A volatile marriage it may have been, but one thing Luca did ensure was that his wife knew how to govern a city. At the time, and easily bored, Sienna had chafed at Luca's daily tutelage but never was she more grateful for his insistence. This invaluable knowledge stood her in excellent stead.

. . .

Aware Sienna had spent a considerable amount of time with Giancarlo del Sabato, her Chief of Security, the chancellor anticipated an announcement of their nuptials sooner rather than later.

Hours of discussions with Giancarlo had convinced Callixtus that the man was a stabilising influence over Sienna's occasionally flighty ways.

He trusted the pair would be dutiful custodians of Florence and, if they weren't, he had plenty of soldiers on standby.

Importantly, with Sophia's input and approval, a mutual defence pact had been agreed between the governors of Rome and Florence, which included official acknowledgement of the Hunters' territory. Sophia had placed Dario in charge of further arbitration should it be necessary.

For the foreseeable future, the upper centre of the peninsula was secure.

In quiet moments, Sophia continued to be haunted by Worthington's allegations. Not brave enough to tackle her mother's journals on her own, she persuaded Bianca to help when the latter called in on her way home to the cottage.

When they unearthed the truth, their abject relief made them giddy and, in one of Noemi's notebooks, a doodle clarified the vague sense of recognition Sophia felt the first time she heard the monsignor's name.

It transpired that the *Ringtonwoth* in *Ringtonwoth Pharmaceuticals* was an anagram of Worthington. Noemi had scribbled pompous prick next to the title, underlining it so many times she scored right through the next three pages.

Further reading revealed Worthington... surprise, surprise... had been somewhat economical with the facts. Despite lacking the expertise to participate in the manufacture of any vaccine, it was *his* error which had corrupted the molecules of a drug Noemi's team was developing to eradicate the building blocks of cancer, resulting in the virulent pathogen.

That he had the audacity to use their mother as a scapegoat for his mistake, incensed the sisters, prompting Sophia to remark that it was a good job Dante had claimed Worthington's head because, "it will make an excellent dart board."

Feeling she ought to admonish the new mother for her grisly humour, Bianca was inclined to agree.

It was early morning.

Callixtus stared out of the window, held in thrall as the rising sun bled life into his ancient and still majestic city.

As the sky morphed from grey through pink and gold to the dazzling cerulean blue, so synonymous with Rome, a contentment, hitherto unknown, suffused his being.

Life was returning to normal... if normal was ever a state which could be used to describe the ongoing chaos that was Rome.

Sophia and her contingent of Hunters had left the previous day with Sienna and the Florentines. A tentative accord, born of circumstance, had blossomed into genuine friendship, with invitations to visit extended from both sides.

The palace seemed somehow smaller and less bright without them but, although hosting so many guests was fun... for a while... Callixtus savoured the tranquillity.

Time enough to deal with the accumulated business later.

A cool breeze lifted the drapes and caused his flesh to pebble, prompting him to tighten the belt of his aged but voluminous bathrobe, presented to him by Sophia and Bianca when Dario and he were handfasted.

That the sisters felt able to part with their mother's personal robe, itself a gift from their father, affirmed their desire to unite the Hunters and the Romans into one family, and meant more than words could express.

Noemi raised her daughters well, he mused, aware that the nebulous yet unmistakable strain… the inevitable legacy of labouring to negotiate an enduring peace… had evaporated.

The rattle of pots and pans wrested the chancellor's thoughts from the poetic to the prosaic, and he headed to the source of the sound.

Leaning against the door jamb of the kitchen, he watched his love and consort setting the moka pot on the stove, the marble benchtop covered in the ingredients for a hearty breakfast.

Something about the domesticated scene reminded him of the night the two of them had, over copious cups of coffee, gone behind Sophia's back to plan the raid on Florence.

Curiosity getting the better of him, Callixtus ventured, "Are you ever going to tell Sophia that we urged her into action without her knowing?"

His question was met with an abrupt silence, broken when the thankfully empty skillet Dario was holding slipped to the floor with a loud clatter.

Bending, Dario picked up the pan, hefting it in his hand as he pondered his answer.

"I would rather face an army of Worthington's lunatics, than contend with the padrona of the Hunters." He sent Callixtus a wicked grin.

"Might I suggest, especially if you wish to enjoy a long happy life with me, you take *that* secret to your grave.

"Now, stop worrying about State secrets and come help me with breakfast."

RORI BLEU

With a smattering of riverboat pirates and royalty in her heritage, Rori Bleu's childhood reflected her past. An interest in fairy tales, myth and legend were as important as spirited discussions around politics and current affairs — although some might argue they are one and the same!

A fascination, sparked by listening to Grimm's Fairy Tales at her grandmother's knee, not only encouraged Rori's passion for reading, but also steered her into the world of RPG's. What began as a fun pastime, soon evolved into the creation of fantastical worlds, but Rori never lost her love of politics going on to specialise in Governmental History and Historical Research.

Naturally this means her stories are steeped in historical accuracy and real-life intrigue. While Rori's love of a happily ever after means her preferred genre is romance, don't be surprised if you discover an occasional detour into historical fiction, thrillers, horror and fantasy.

ROSIE CHAPEL

Rosie Chapel lives in Perth, Australia with her hubby and two furkids. When not writing, she loves catching up with friends, burying herself in a book (or three), discovering the wonders of Western Australia, or — and the best — a quiet evening at home with her husband, enjoying a glass of wine and a movie.

Website: www.rosiechapel.com

ALSO BY RORI BLEU

Pineapple Meringue

Imprisoned Hearts

Port of London

Dani's Masquerade

Black Tulips

Ajei's Destiny

Porta Aeternum

The Queen's Heart

Syn *with Matthew Forester*

*****

With Rosie Chapel

Echoes and Illusions - The Hunters: Book 1

Evie's War

Vindicta

Corrupt Covenant

Lesser of Two Evils

Deadly Incision

The Sela Helsdatter Saga

A Flip of The Coin - Book One

Conceived Chaos - Book Two

Odin's Bane - Book Three

Valhalla's Doom - Book Four

Arcane Alchemy: Freya's Fate - *A Helsdatter Saga Novella*

ALSO BY ROSIE CHAPEL

Historical Fiction

The Hannah's Heirloom Sequence

The Pomegranate Tree - Book One

Echoes of Stone and Fire - Book Two

Embers of Destiny - Book Three

Etched in Starlight - Prequel

Hannah's Heirloom Trilogy - Compilation — e-book only

Prelude to Fate

Legacy of Flame and Ash

The Nettleby Trilogy (WW1 Novellas)

A Guardian Unexpected - Book One

Under the Clock - Book Two

Between Heartbeats - Book Three

Regency Romances

The Linen and Lace Series

Once Upon An Earl - Book One

To Unlock Her Heart - Book Two

Love on a Winter's Tide - Book Three

A Love Unquenchable - Book Four

A Hidden Rose — Book Five

An Unexpected Romance

Elusive Hearts - Book One

Shrouded Hearts - Book Two

The Daffodil Garden

The Unconventional Duchess

Rescuing Her Knight - *the de Wiltons:* Book One

His Fiery Hoyden

A Regency Duet

A Regency Christmas Double

Fate is Curious

A Christmas Prayer *with Ashlee Shades*

The Lady's Wager

Winning Emma

A Love Impossible

Unravelling Roana

Love Kindled

Moonbeams and Mistletoe

Fairy Tale Romance

Chasing Bluebells

Contemporary Romances

Of Ruins and Romance

All At Once It's You

Cobweb Dreams

Just One Step

His Heart's Second Sigh

*****

With Rori Bleu

Echoes & Illusions - The Hunters: Book 1

Evie's War

Vindicta

Corrupt Covenant

Lesser of Two Evils

Deadly Incision

The Sela Helsdatter Saga

A Flip of The Coin - Book One

Conceived Chaos - Book Two

Odin's Bane - Book Three

Valhalla's Doom - Book Four

Arcane Alchemy: Freya's Fate - *A Helsdatter Saga Novella*